DYLAN'S DADDY DILEMMA

BY
TRACY MADISON

Published in Great Britain 2015
by Mills & Boon, an imprint of Harlequin (UK) Limited,
Eton House, 18-24 Paradise Road, Richmond, Surrey, TW9 1SR

© 2015 Tracy Leigh Ritts

ISBN: 978-0-263-25146-3

23-0615

Printed and bound in Spain
by CPI Barc...

Tracy Madison is an award-winning author who makes her home in northwestern Ohio. As a wife and a mother, her days are filled with love, laughter and many cups of coffee. She often spends her nights awake and at the keyboard, bringing her characters to life and leading them toward their well-deserved happily-ever-afters, one word at a time. Tracy loves to hear from readers. You can reach her at tracy@tracymadison.com.

To my darling, sweet Arabella,
whose smile outshines the sun.

Chapter One

Now what? Defeated and drained, Chelsea Bell tugged on her four-year-old son's hand and led them toward the battered, almost-out-of-gas Chevy Malibu that had brought them the 260-plus miles from Pueblo to Steamboat Springs, Colorado.

Henry didn't ask why they were returning to the car, just shuffled alongside her, his spare body bowed against the chilly wind. Surprising, really, when just minutes ago she'd promised that they were done driving for a while, and that this beautiful A-frame house with its amazing mountain views was their new—albeit, temporary—home.

The house-sitting job had been exactly what she needed for a fresh start. A roof over their heads and decent pay for close to five months meant she'd have plenty of time to locate permanent employment and a small, affordable place to live when the seasonal gig ended in September. Unfortunately, seconds after knocking on the front door, she'd learned that they'd come all this way for nothing. The job was gone, given to someone else.

A solid portion of bad luck, timing and her own poor judgment were to blame.

First, her car had malfunctioned, requiring last-minute repairs the mechanic had deemed nothing more than Band-Aids. He'd strongly suggested she junk the car and put her money toward something newer. Of course, she couldn't afford newer, so she'd gone with the short-term fix and used a chunk of her not-so-healthy savings in the process.

Then Henry had awakened with the flu on the day they were supposed to leave, delaying them further. She'd called her would-be employers twice before her pay-as-you-go phone had run out of minutes, had left messages but hadn't actually spoken with them. And seeing how she'd spent so much to fix her car and didn't trust it wouldn't break down again, she'd decided to conserve her drastically dwindling funds rather than adding more minutes.

She should have bought the minutes, because when the home owners attempted to reach her and found her phone out of service, they'd assumed she'd bailed. A logical assumption under the circumstances, and one she likely would have made in a similar situation. Understanding the whys, however, didn't change her current predicament one iota.

There were no two ways about it. She was good and stuck.

Shivering as much from her jagged emotions as the cold, late-winter weather, Chelsea opened the door to the backseat. "Hop in, kid," she said in as cheery a voice as she could muster. "Seems our plans have changed. How does dinner sound? I bet you're hungry."

"I thought we were staying here." Henry crawled into the safety booster seat and tiredly rubbed his eyes. Unlike most kids, he never slept well in the car, so the long drive had worn him out. Her, too, but she'd grown accustomed to exhaustion. "I don't wanna drive anymore."

"We're not going far," she promised. "I saw several restaurants in the center of town. I was thinking we could stop for burgers and fries." After buckling him in, she tousled the top of his sandy-brown-covered head. "Unless you'd rather have another peanut-butter sandwich?"

In an effort to save for this trip, their menu for the past many weeks had largely consisted of peanut-butter sandwiches. She had little doubt her son would jump at the chance to eat his favorite dinner in a real restaurant. An extravagance she absolutely couldn't afford, but the kid had to eat and she needed the break to decide what they should do next.

"Burgers!" Henry's face lit up in a megawatt smile. "And a root beer!"

"Milk," she countered. "You had a soda when we stopped for gas."

"Juice?"

"Milk," she repeated before closing his door. Always the negotiator, that was her son. She slid into her seat and with a silent prayer put the key into the ignition. The engine balked, hacking and coughing itself awake before settling into its normal state of aggravated compliance. She backed out of the driveway with a sigh of relief.

Henry remained quiet as they drove, likely due to a combination of fatigue and contemplation over the milk debate. Breathing deeply, Chelsea tried to ignore the heavy pressure on her chest. This was bad. Really bad. Other than Henry—who counted on her to make his world safe—she was alone in a strange city with little cash and nowhere to go.

Tears stung her eyes as the reality of her dilemma sank in.

Should they turn around and return to Pueblo? She didn't have to look in her wallet to know it held one crumpled five-dollar bill and two twenties. There were a couple of ones in her coat pocket and probably a handful of change lurking in the bottom of her purse. All told, she had less than fifty dollars to her name. Enough, maybe, to get them back to Pueblo. If she drove straight through and her car didn't gasp its last breath en route. But why?

She'd spend most—if not all—of her cash in the process, and frankly, there wasn't much of anything left for them in Pueblo. No home. No job. No true friendships. Henry's father—if anyone dared call Joel Marin that— had walked into the sunset shortly after learning she was pregnant. For most of Henry's life, she hadn't heard one peep from him, but six months ago, she'd received a post-card—a damn postcard, mailed from California—with a scrawled "Was thinking of you and wanted to say hi!"

Really? Close to five years, zero communication, zero support, zero interest in Henry, and he sent her that? And how had he gotten her address?

She didn't know, but she'd thrown the postcard into the trash and had put him and it out of her mind. Then, two months ago, she'd heard he was back in Pueblo. He hadn't shown up on her doorstep, so she'd assumed he didn't want to see Henry, but just knowing they were in the same city was enough for her to decide to pick up stakes and move on.

Plainly speaking, she wanted nothing to do with Joel Marin. Ever again. And she felt more emphatically about keeping Joel away from Henry. Her son deserved better than a fly-by-night, immature man who had bolted from his responsibilities as a father. The fact Joel was now in Pueblo only added a check mark to the con side of her what-to-do-next list.

And what remained of Chelsea's family—save her sister, but Lindsay had her own set of problems—would just as soon hang up on her than offer their help.

So. She could be broke, alone and homeless in Pueblo

and deal with the remote possibility of Joel popping into her life, or *almost* broke, alone and homeless in Steamboat Springs, but without the worry of Joel hanging over her head.

Inappropriate laughter bubbled in her chest. When thought of like that, the choice was pretty damn simple. Sad and scary, but simple. She'd rather save the money she had and take her chances here than head back to a place she couldn't wait to leave.

Okay, then. One decision made. Now she just had to find a new fresh start. She'd done it before and she could do so again.

"You win, Mommy," Henry said from the backseat. "I'll drink the milk."

"You will, huh? That's good to hear."

"Yup! *Chocolate* milk!"

She almost argued, but decided to give in on this front. "I think we can make that happen." Amused despite the weight of her fears, Chelsea braked at a stop sign. Her son's tenacious, never-give-up attitude always reminded her of what was important. Even when the world seemed bent on crumbling around them. So, yeah, he'd get his chocolate milk, and she'd keep them safe. Somehow. "Thank you, Henry."

"For what?"

"Oh, I don't know. Just for being you."

Henry laughed, and the normalcy—the joy—of that sound wove into her heart and rekindled her hope. "I like being me," he said, "so it's easy. And fun!"

And that, Chelsea thought as she pulled into the parking lot of a place called Foster's Pub and Grill, was a motto everyone should live by.

Dylan Foster winked at the curvaceous blonde who'd flirted mercilessly with him ever since sitting down at the bar an hour earlier. She'd started off with a beer before moving on to a rum and Diet Coke, and had just ordered a Snowshoe shooter, which consisted of bourbon whiskey and peppermint schnapps. Three drinks in an hour didn't cause him concern—he'd obviously seen far quicker consumption rates—nor did the relatively quick uptick in the alcohol percentage in each successive drink bother him all that much.

What worried Dylan was the look in the blonde's eyes. He'd tended bar at his family's establishment long enough to recognize when someone was on a mission, and unless he was completely off base, this woman was bent on retaliation. Probably due to some man doing something stupid and ticking her off. Or breaking her heart. Or, he supposed, both.

And he drew these conclusions based on the mix of sorrow and heat in her gaze, her relentless come-ons toward him and the guy sitting next to her—hedging her bets, he assumed—and finally, the way she kept looking over her shoulder toward the pub's entrance. Waiting for the husband or boyfriend to show up and find her drunk-happy with some other guy.

Not him. He wasn't interested in a one-night, two-night or any-number-of-nights stand. But the man seated on the bar stool to the left of the blonde had responded eagerly to her not-so-subtle advances. Which could then mean a potential fight if and when Mr. Heartbreaker chose to make an appearance. So, yep, Dylan was concerned.

Foster's Pub and Grill was, more than anything else, a restaurant that housed a bar. Sure, they'd had their share of rowdy gatherings, and they would again. Typically, though, they were a casual place for the tourists and locals alike to grab a meal, a few drinks and kick back after a day on the slopes. Or after hours of hiking or white-water rafting during the summer season.

He never relished the idea of trouble, but seeing how tonight was one of the last before the winter season ended, he was damn tired. He just didn't have the energy for trouble. So he winked at the blonde to draw her attention from her other prey, hoping she'd focus on him and forget about Mr. Miller Lite long enough for the guy to seek out greener pastures.

Or just give up and leave. Either would suit Dylan. His plan beyond that was sketchy, but he figured he'd be able to contain the situation, assuming one presented itself, if he removed as many unpredictable factors as possible.

He winked again for good measure and slid the shooter across the surface of the bar. "There you go," he said. "Might want to slow down a bit after this one."

"I have no intentions of slowing down," the blonde said, accepting the shooter and downing it in one long gulp. "And I don't have to drive tonight, so…another, please."

Dylan considered cutting her off, but he didn't really have a legit reason. Her words were clear and she wasn't swaying in her seat, and she'd just stated that she wasn't planning on driving. So he went about making her another Snowshoe.

"Anyone ever tell you how sexy your eyes are?" she asked when he set the drink in front of her. "What color are they, exactly? Green…brown…hazel?"

"Depends on the day," he said, answering her second question. Both he and his younger sister, Haley, shared their Irish mother's coloring, including her chameleon eyes and brown hair with, in the summer, glints of red. Haley called the color auburn. Dylan preferred the simpler description of plain old brown. His older brother, Reid, and younger brother, Cole, took after their father, sporting almost-black eyes and hair. "And, I've been told, my mood."

"Ooh," the woman said. "And what might your mood be right now?"

Before an appropriate response—one that couldn't be taken as too flirtatious—presented itself, the door to the pub opened, snagging his and the blonde's attention. Not the heartbreaker, Dylan was relieved to see, but a young boy who all but tumbled into the restaurant, followed closely by, presumably, his mother. Even from across the room, both appeared windblown and out of sorts. Tired, too, if the woman's hunched shoulders were anything to go by.

Grasping her son's hand, the woman pulled him farther into the restaurant and, after searching the area for an empty table, headed toward their solitary choice: a tiny two-seater near the bar. They removed their coats and sat down, and the woman—a tall, too-thin brunette—closed her eyes and let out a long breath. Not just tired, Dylan amended, but exhausted.

Far more curious than he should be, he grabbed a couple of menus from under the bar and, with an easy grin directed at the blonde, said, "Duty calls."

"Hurry back," she said, batting her mascara-coated lashes at top speed. "I'm almost ready for another drink, and you haven't answered my question yet."

Question? Oh, about his *mood*. Seeing how his solitary goal was to go home—*alone*—and sleep until ten tomorrow morning, he doubted she'd like his response. Rather than saying anything, he nodded and made his escape. As he approached the table where the brunette and the child were, he tried to convince himself that he wasn't interested in the least.

He was just lending a hand. Foster's was short staffed tonight, and Haley—who normally worked behind the scenes in the office—was working double duty by waiting tables. At the moment, she had a tray balanced on each arm and was maneuvering a path around the packed tables toward an extralarge group of customers.

Nothing wrong with easing his sister's load a little.

Believable enough, Dylan supposed, except for the fact that Haley was a damn fine waitress. She'd see and attend to the new arrivals soon enough. Why, then, did he feel compelled to deliver the menus himself? Especially when he had a full bar to contend with and his worrisome pre-monition that the flirty blonde was trouble? Didn't matter.

He'd drop off the menus, tell the brunette and the boy about the evening's specials, and that would be that. Haley could take over from there.

"Evening," he said when he reached their table and had handed them their menus. "We have several specials going on tonight, including—"

"I want a hamburger and root beer, but Mommy says I have to have milk," the boy interrupted, his excitement obvious. "So chocolate milk and French fries. With dip!"

"Ranch dressing," his mother supplied. "And the burger should be well-done, with nothing on it except for cheese and mustard. Do you… Is there a kid-size burger?"

"Yup, there is," Dylan answered, fighting the urge to grin at the child's exuberance. Heck, the rascal was so jazzed, he kept bouncing in his seat. It was cute. Pulling the order pad from the pocket of his apron, Dylan focused on the mother. She was cute, too. "What about you? Do you need a minute to look over the menu, or would you like to hear the specials?"

The question seemed, oddly, to fluster the woman. She dipped her chin so she was looking at the table rather than at Dylan. "Oh. I…already ate. Maybe a cup of coffee?"

"That's not true," the boy said with a curious glance to-ward his mother. "Not since before we left for the brand-new fresh start this morning. I remember. You had a peanut-butter sandwich and a glass of water and you didn't even eat when I did at lunch."

"Henry, I'm…" She trailed off, lifted her head and shrugged at her son. "I guess you're right, but I'm not that hungry, so—" she returned her gaze to Dylan "—just the coffee, please."

"Sure," Dylan said, jotting down the order. The action gave him a second to consider the give-and-take he'd just witnessed. That, along with the dark circles under the brunette's eyes and the exhaustion he'd already recognized, made him think she was in some sort of a jam. Not that he should care one way or the other. Not his business. "Coffee it is, then. How do you take it?"

"Cream, no sugar."

"Kitchen is busy, so the wait might be slightly longer than normal," he said. "I'll have someone bring a bread basket, free of charge, to compensate."

"That isn't necessary."

"Nope, it isn't. But it's what we do." And with that, he turned on his heel and walked away before he could offer her a free meal to boot. Because dammit, that was what he wanted to do, and the want made no sense. He did not swoop in to save damsels in distress. Not anymore. Not for a long, long time. Besides which, maybe she really wasn't that hungry or in a jam.

Maybe, for once, he'd completely misinterpreted the signals.

"This is *so* good," Henry said, dipping the very last French fry into a shallow bowl of ranch dressing. "I like our fresh start so far." Squinting his eyes, he quickly revised his statement by saying "Now that we're done driving, I mean."

"We are definitely done driving, sweetheart." Chelsea tore off a piece of bread and chewed it slowly. She had been hungry, but Henry's meal, her coffee, plus the tip was already more than she could afford. So despite her earlier refusal, she was grateful for the bread.

Oh, they still had half a jar of peanut bar and a loaf of bread in the car, along with packages of crackers and cereal bars and a few juice boxes. She wouldn't have actually starved without the bread basket, but she likely wouldn't have allowed herself to dip into their food supply again until the morning. After all, she didn't know how long it would have to last.

While Henry had eaten his burger, she'd gathered the stray dollars from her coat pocket and the loose change from the bottom of her purse. Now, at least, she had a total. They had forty-seven dollars and seventy-two cents to work with. That was it. And when she paid their bill here, she'd have thirty-seven dollars and twenty-two cents left.

She might have to swallow her pride and reach out for help. Her choices were few. Lindsay, maybe, if Chelsea could contact her sister without her husband's knowledge. Risky, though. Kirk was a carbon copy of their father—a guy who believed women existed for the sole purpose of doing a man's bidding—and he controlled nearly every aspect of Lindsay's life. Because Chelsea recognized this about Kirk and had attempted to talk her sister out of marrying him, Kirk did everything possible to keep the sisters apart.

Mostly, he'd managed to do so. For whatever reason, her sister refused to see the truth. Even so, she loved Chelsea. She'd send whatever money she could, but Chelsea did not want to cause more problems. Better for everyone involved if she kept her sister out of this mess.

That left Melissa. A friend, but not a close one. Chelsea's fault, as she never allowed anyone to get too close, but Melissa had always been kind. They'd both worked as waitresses, usually on the same shift at an all-night diner, and less than two weeks ago, Melissa had hugged Chelsea and asked her to keep in touch. A kind woman, yes, but how could she ask for assistance from another single mother who was already fighting to make ends meet?

Melissa would likely try to help, but knowing her circumstances meant that Chelsea shouldn't ask. Sighing, she shook her head. No, it meant she *wouldn't*. The decision had zip to do with pride. She'd gotten herself into this situation; she'd have to find a path through to the other side. Without calling on her sister or Melissa.

And that put her exactly where she'd started, where she'd purposely put herself time and again: alone. Without a safety net or a solitary person to lean on, or even a plan B.

For the first time in a long while, Chelsea wished she hadn't built such a solid, impenetrable wall around herself and that she'd let one trustworthy person into her life. The problem, she knew, was in order to determine if a person was trustworthy, you first had to risk that they weren't. Which then allowed them close enough access to cause some serious damage.

In her experience, the risk had never paid off. But if she'd been luckier, and if such a person existed in her life, maybe she wouldn't feel so inadequate and alone right now.

Desperation clawed in Chelsea's stomach. Her only true priority for the past four and a half years had been Henry. Every decision she made had his best interests at heart and now…well, she'd failed at keeping her son safe. And unless she could find a motel in Steamboat Springs that only charged ten dollars for a night's stay, they'd be sleeping in the car.

Oh, God. No. Just…no.

Instructing herself to breathe, to calm the churning

panic so she could think without emotion, she focused straight ahead and saw the man who'd brought them their menus.

Tall and lithely muscular, he worked the bar with an ease that spoke of years of experience. Somehow, watching his quick, seemingly effortless movements softened the tightness in her chest. It was a reprieve of sorts, so she continued to watch as he prepared and delivered drinks, as he smiled and chatted and sometimes laughed to those he served. She envied him and his obvious comfort in his surroundings. In his life.

When had she last felt such a sense of security and acceptance?

Not since her grandmother Sophia had passed when she was thirteen. Before then, Sophia had been Chelsea's refuge, her home and her haven. From her parents, her sadness, her…well, just about everything else back then. But Sophia couldn't help her now.

In that second, Chelsea came to the conclusion that she would *never* be in this position again. No matter what it took. No matter what she had to do. And the first order of business was securing a safe, warm place for her and Henry to sleep for the night. Tomorrow, when the sun rose, she would scour the entire city until she found a job.

Any job, really. Anything that would get her from this point to the next.

"I'll be right back," she said to Henry. "Just sit tight."

"Where are you going?" He stopped playing with his straw and sat up straight, worry dotting his expression. "I want to come with you."

"I know, but if you wait here, we won't lose our table." True, perhaps, but that wasn't Chelsea's concern. She didn't want her son to know how desperate a position they were in. "I'm going up there," she said, pointing in the direction of the bar. "We'll be able to see each other the entire time. I won't be long, and if you get nervous, you can come to me. Okay?"

"Okay," he agreed after a momentary pause.

Leaning over, she gave him a quick kiss on the top of his head. Then, with hopes of a miracle, she approached the well-polished vintage oak bar. Again, she focused on the bartender, on his relaxed smile and his easy, almost graceful, movements. If a cheap—okay, almost *free*— motel existed in Steamboat Springs, he'd surely know of it, and if she were very lucky, he might have some ideas about possible job openings in the area.

Humiliating to ask for any type of help whatsoever— even basic advice—from a stranger. She'd have to tell him some version of the truth, maybe even admit she'd failed, otherwise he wouldn't understand her dilemma. And if he didn't understand, why would he bother himself with giving her anything more than pat answers?

All of this seemed too much, too overwhelming, and she almost retreated. *Almost.* But her earlier promise to do whatever it took strengthened her resolve. She marched forward and readied the words she'd have to say.

Because really, what else was she to do?

Chapter Two

The weight of her gaze struck him a millisecond before the sound of her voice, causing Dylan to overfill the pilsner. Frustrated with himself, he poured off some of the foam and wiped the side of the glass with the rag tucked into the waistband of his apron.

Would this night *ever* come to an end? He'd been off balance for the past hour, ever since handing the menus to the brunette and her kid. Not only did the out-of-character behavior hold zero logic, but it was annoying as hell. He didn't appreciate having his head filled with curiosity *and* concern for absolute strangers. No matter how cute they were.

"Excuse me?" the brunette said again, louder this time, as he turned in her direction. "I was wondering if I could ask you a few questions? About—"

"Kind of busy at the moment," he said, a tad more bluntly than he'd anticipated. Chagrined, he forced a smile. "But sure. Just give me a minute."

"Of course," she said. "No problem."

A solid ten minutes later, after he'd delivered the beer and two others, paused to chat with the blonde—who was now on her fourth shooter, but at least she'd taken to sipping instead of gulping—and cleaned up a couple of spills, he returned to where the brunette waited.

She stood in such a way that she could watch both her boy and Dylan, and therefore, she saw him coming. "I can see you're busy," she said when he stopped in front of her. "And I'm sorry to bother you, but I need…well, some advice. I'm guessing you're from around here?"

"No bother, and that I am," he said. "What can I do for you?"

A rosy blush colored her cheeks, easily visible even in the dim lighting. "We just got here today, and it was supposed to be for a job. It…um… The job fell through. So, I'm wondering if you can direct me to a motel that isn't too pricey? We're not picky."

Prickly dots of tension appeared between Dylan's shoulder blades. He found no pleasure in hearing his assumptions were right on the money, but he choked down the questions her statement raised. Namely, why come for a job—whether it fell through or not—without having a place to stay? Seemed foolish and shortsighted, especially with a child to consider.

"That might be tough. This is the last weekend the mountain is open, so the city's packed with tourists. It's doubtful you'll have any luck in finding a hotel with vacancies, cheap or not." He should've left it at that, but he didn't. Couldn't, really. "I can grab the phone book and circle a few possibilities, if you like. Doesn't hurt to check."

She nodded her thanks and swung her gaze toward her son. In the instant before she did, Dylan recognized distress in her eyes. Beautiful eyes, deep blue in color and framed in long, dark lashes. Eyes that shouldn't, under any circumstances, be coated with fear.

Another idiotic, out-of-character thought. Shaking it off, Dylan retrieved the phone book and hurriedly circled the three cheapest motels he knew of that weren't dumps. With that and the bar phone in hand, he set them down in front of her. "There you go," he said, his voice capturing her attention. "If you need anything else, let me know."

"Actually, I was also wondering if you knew of any places that might be hiring? We're here now, so I thought we might as well stay." Again, her cheeks darkened in embarrassment. "It's a long drive back to where we came from. It seems pointless to turn around."

He opened his mouth, set to tell her the truth: this was a bad weekend to be looking for work in Steamboat Springs. Most of the local businesses would be doing the same as Foster's, which was skimming down their seasonal employee load until the summer rush began.

Except he couldn't. The fear he'd witnessed seconds ago stopped him in his tracks.

"Let me give that one some thought," he said instead, unwilling to dash her hopes so quickly. Ridiculous, though. The truth remained the truth. "Why don't you make the calls, figure out where you're sleeping for the night, and I'll see what I can come up with?"

Relief mixed with gratitude—maybe even some surprise—softened her smile, relaxing the angled features of her face. "Thank you," she said, her words quiet and hesitant. "My name is Chelsea, by the way. And my son is Henry."

"Nice to meet you. I'm Dylan Foster."

With that, he moved to the other end of the bar, making the sweep to see who needed what drink and who wanted to close out their tab. As he did, he considered her request, trying to come up with at least one job possibility to offer. Foster's Pub wasn't hiring. Neither was the other Foster family–owned business, the sporting-goods store his brother Cole managed.

So lost was he in these thoughts, his appraisal of the bar's customers and their needs, he failed to pay adequate attention to the blonde. It was the sound of her laughter— a series of too loud, too playful, completely manufactured giggles—that yanked him clean out of his head and smack into the trouble he'd anticipated the whole damn evening.

It didn't take an abundance of brainpower to size up the current situation. She had scooted herself closer to Mr. Miller Lite—so close she might as well have plopped herself on his lap—and was in the process of trailing her long red-painted fingernails down the front of his shirt. The poor sucker had his arm wrapped around her waist and was, by all appearances, clueless as to what was about to go down. Because coming toward the couple in long, heavy strides was another man—Mr. Heartbreaker, Dylan guessed—and he did not look pleased.

The blonde seemed quite content with herself and the blowout that was likely to occur. Dylan rushed forward, intent on stopping the altercation before it started and mentally cursing himself for allowing the brunette—Chelsea? Yeah, that was her name—to take over his thoughts. If not for her sad, fearful blue eyes, he would've been on top of this a hell of a lot sooner.

He stepped in front of the blonde at the same instant Mr. Heartbreaker arrived behind the couple. Bad luck, that, but Dylan smiled at the man and said, "What can I get for you?"

The man ignored Dylan. He grabbed Mr. Miller Lite's arm and pulled it off the blonde's waist, saying, "It's time to go, Amber. You've made your point."

"Oh, I don't know that I have." Excitement glimmered over her expression, there and gone in a blink. Facing the new arrival, she said, "Ask me tomorrow. And I'm not going anywhere with you. Now or ever. So you're wasting your time."

"Hold on here," Mr. Miller Lite said. "Who is this guy? What's this about, Amber?"

"His name is Brett, but there's nothing to worry about," Amber said, pressing her body another inch tighter against Mr. Miller Lite, her words a catlike purr. "He doesn't have to ruin our fun or our night. He was just leaving."

"We're leaving together," Brett the heartbreaker corrected. "And tomorrow, we'll straighten all of this out, when you're more willing to listen to reason."

"Reason? I highly doubt there is anything—" She broke off, bit her bottom lip in a sultry type of pout. "Just leave."

"You heard her," Mr. Miller Lite said, disentangling himself from Amber so he could stand. "She doesn't want to go with you—" he curled his fists at his sides "—so why don't you stop embarrassing yourself and take off before someone gets hurt?"

Amber's eyes widened and Brett's mouth pursed into a glower. Uh-oh.

"Let's all calm down. This seems like a private discussion," Dylan interjected, considering how fast he'd be able to climb over the bar and physically get in between the two men and wishing that one of his brothers were also in attendance. Or, hell, both. "And this isn't the place for a private discussion, so I think everyone should—"

That was all he managed to say before the first punch was thrown.

As far as fights went, Dylan had seen worse. Brett got two solid hits in, a clean one across Mr. Miller Lite's jaw and the other straight into the gut. Mr. Miller Lite retaliated with an elbow punch, also to the gut, followed by several sharp jabs to the ribs. Brett was raring up for another go when Dylan and a couple of the pub's employees managed to separate the two. From what he could see, no real damage was done, though both men would surely have a few bruises the next day. And, he was certain, very different stories to tell.

Fortunately, when Amber sidled next to Brett, obviously ready to mend fences, Mr. Miller Lite was smart enough not to argue. Dylan shooed him out first, and a few minutes later he sent Brett and Amber on their way. He didn't know what had started their squabble, but he figured this wasn't their first—nor would it be their last—go-around. They just had that look.

"The show is over, folks," he said to the gawkers who hadn't yet returned to their seats. None of whom had jumped in to help during the fight, thank goodness. That would have resulted in one hell of a mess. Everyone scattered to their various chairs, and within minutes the fight was forgotten and normalcy was restored.

It wasn't until the hum of chatter had fully resumed that Dylan recalled Chelsea and her plight. *Dammit.* Nothing had changed. The facts were still the facts. There might be plenty of job openings in the city, but he didn't know where, and really, that was fine. She was an adult and, despite the effect she'd had on him, a complete stranger. He had no business being concerned.

She wasn't—in any way, shape or form—his responsibility.

Except when he searched the bar for her and her son and didn't see them anywhere, knots formed in his stomach. Had she found a hotel? She'd mentioned they'd driven a long way, so he guessed she wouldn't turn around for the return trip tonight, even if she had made the decision to leave. And honestly, if she didn't have a job and had nowhere to go, why choose to stay?

Shaking off his absurd worries—why the devil did he care, anyway?—Dylan returned to working the bar and socializing with the customers. He refused to waste another second thinking about some woman he'd likely never see or hear from again.

The next several hours passed swiftly, and finally— thank God—it was closing time. Another hour spent putting the bar to rights and he was heading out through the kitchen, ready to go home and crash for a solid eight. Nine, if he could get away with it.

Haley was still in the kitchen, eating a late-night snack at the small round table the family and employees used. He grabbed a chair and sat down across from her, because as much as he wanted to hightail it home, he wouldn't let his sister walk to her car alone.

"Long night," she said in between bites of a turkey sandwich. "Long season."

"Agreed. We're almost done, though." One more night of craziness and everything would calm down for a few months. Of course, as soon as he caught up on sleep and fun, boredom would settle in. It always did. "Any plans I should know about on your end?"

"Huh? Me? Nope." She shrugged, twirled a lock of hair around her finger. "Nothing exciting, anyway. I mean, nothing that *you* would find exciting."

"Is that so?"

"Yep, that's so." She twirled her hair tighter. "Just the normal in-between-season stuff."

Dylan tried to find the energy to question his sister further, because she was—without a doubt—hiding something. The twirling of her hair, one of Haley's tells, was a dead giveaway, but she could keep her secret. She was in a good place in her life. For well over a year now—closing in on two, actually—she'd been happy and in love with a man the entire Foster family considered one of their own. Whatever her secret, he highly doubted there was reason for alarm.

"Okay, then," he said. "Please tell me you're almost done with that sandwich."

Narrowing her more-green-than-brown-tonight eyes, she gave him a protracted once-over. "Are you okay? You didn't get your head beat on while breaking up that fight, did you?"

"Can't win with you, Haley," he joked. "Either I ask too many questions or not enough. I'm fine. Just tired and cranky and ready to head home."

"Then go! What are you waiting for?"

He gave her a pointed look. "You. Finish eating so I can walk you out."

"Oh. You don't have to. Gavin dropped me off earlier, and he'll be here to get me soon." After swallowing another bite, she said, "I just called him. So no worries, big brother."

"You're sure?"

"I'm sure. He enjoys—" she smiled widely, happily "—picking me up."

Dylan laughed at the innuendo, mostly to hide his reflexive wince of discomfort. Didn't matter how much he liked Gavin, Haley would always be his baby sister. Some days he still saw her in pigtails. "I'm sure he does."

After saying their good-nights, he walked outside and strode toward his parked car, which he'd left in the very back part of the lot. Cold wind smacked against his face in waves, so he tugged his coat collar up and over his jaw for protection. The air held the icy-crisp sharpness of winter, making it difficult to believe they were easing into spring.

He was about halfway across the parking lot when he heard the coughing, choking, sputtering sounds of an engine desperately trying to turn over. A stranded customer? Probably. A local, he'd guess, since tourists tended to rent vehicles, and typically those cars were newer and didn't emit cries of impending death when started.

Stopping, he waited and hoped the engine would fire to life and he'd be free to go on his merry way. But nope, no such luck. The sputtering continued in growls and grunts, the gap in between each cough growing systematically longer by several seconds. In a matter of minutes, Dylan guessed, the car would become completely unresponsive.

Ah, hell. This he did not need.

But because his folks had raised him to lend a hand when one was needed, he switched his direction. Maybe the car just required a jump, which he could do without too much effort. If not, he'd lead the stranded person inside and wait with them until a tow truck arrived.

He approached the car—a decade-plus-old Chevy Malibu, he now saw—and grimaced at the now grinding, winding-down sound of an engine giving up the ghost. The driver needed to stop his attempts, because no amount of key turning and gas-pedal pumping was going to do the trick. And while he hated to admit it, he had serious doubts that the issue was the relatively simple matter of a battery requiring a jump.

This night seriously did not want to end.

Hungry, tired and…okay, irritated, Dylan paused mere inches from the car as recognition hit. His heart dropped clear to his stomach, because naturally, the person sitting behind the wheel frantically twisting the key in the ignition was none other than the too-skinny tall brunette who had consumed his thoughts for the majority of the evening. Chelsea.

And behind her, stretched out on the backseat, curled up in a blanket—and from his vantage point, apparently asleep—was her son, Henry. Dylan swore under his breath, knowing instinctively that she hadn't found a hotel and that her convoluted plan was to spend the night in this behemoth of a car that now refused to start.

No heat. No safety. No nothing. Just an unprotected

woman with her young child, sleeping in their car in a strange city on a cold, windy night with nowhere else to go. And his irritation climbed to a whole new level.

Striding forward, he raised his fist and knocked on the driver-side window. She froze before looking at him through the glass, her expression stricken at his sudden presence. Which meant, despite the glow from the parking-lot lights, she hadn't seen or even sensed his approach. Pushing out a breath, reining in his annoyance, he gestured for her to roll down her window.

After a moment's hesitation, she did.

"That car is dead in the water," he said before she could utter a solitary syllable. "And even if it wasn't, you can't sleep there. It isn't safe."

"Who said I was sleeping here?" she responded, her tone strong and defensive. Well, he couldn't blame her for either. As far as she knew, he was a bad guy. "And I always have trouble with the car when it's cold outside, but I'm sure it will start. So we're fine."

She thought she was fine? Dylan bit back the curse he almost muttered and shook his head in resignation. He downgraded his hopeful nine hours of sleep to an adequate seven and jammed his hands into his coat pockets to fend off frozen fingers.

In a measured, calm meter, he said, "The last thing you are is fine."

"The car will start." Her chin firmed in stubbornness. "It's just…temperamental in cold climates."

"Uh-huh." Weighing his next move, he thought of and discarded several reasonable arguments. He did not want to cause her undue alarm, but he also wasn't about to walk off and leave her and her kid alone. "If you think you can get that car to run, I'll wait right here while you do," he said. "Then, since you said you're not sleeping here, I assume that means you have somewhere else to go, so I'll drive behind you to ascertain your car doesn't become… temperamental again and leave you stranded."

"You can go. I'm good," she said hurriedly. "None of that is necessary."

"In my book, all of it is necessary. Or," he said, hoping he was wrong about the sleeping-in-the-car business, "I can call you a cab. You'll be on your way in no time. Your choice."

"No. I… The car *will* start."

"I don't think it will."

She didn't respond, just turned the key again…and then again…to no avail. "Come on," she murmured before trying a third time. This attempt yielded a sharp, whining gasp.

"Don't try again," he warned. "Just—"

Chelsea swore and twisted the key once more. Nothing. Not a cough or a whine or a hack. Her shoulders trembled and she inhaled a deep breath. Several seconds elapsed before she looked at him, and when she did, her eyes were shiny with the promise of tears. Oh, hell.

"I didn't find a hotel I can afford," she admitted in a quiet, defeated voice that matched every inch of her body language. "And maybe the car won't start until it warms up some tomorrow, but we'll be fine. I have a ton of blankets and…and…"

"Get your son and get out of the car," Dylan said before the promise of tears became a reality. That, he knew, would be his complete undoing. "I'll carry whatever else you need. But you're sure as hell not sleeping out here tonight."

Doubt and fear clouded her gaze, her voice. "That isn't a good idea."

"Do you have a better one?" No response. Dylan counted to three, and then to five. He understood, even admired, her reluctance. But something had to give to change the status quo. "Look," he said, "I get it. This is an awkward situation and you don't know me from Adam, but you'll have to trust that my only goal here is to get some shut-eye. That won't happen if I leave you and your son on a friggin' cold night that will only get colder. Let me help. Please."

"I appreciate your kindness, but…" She squinted her eyes in assessment. Of him and, probably, the veracity of his words. She gave a quick, decisive shake to her head. "It's a generous offer, but I have to decline. It's better, I think, if we stay here and wait for morning."

"That's—" He clamped his jaw shut before uttering the word *idiotic*. She was, after all, only trying to remain safe. She wasn't going to budge and he wouldn't—couldn't—leave her and her kid out here alone, vulnerable to the weather and other unpredictable, possibly dangerous, factors. "All righty, then. You win," he said, settling on the one remaining, uncomfortable-as-all-get-out alternative and pointing toward his parked car on the other side of the lot. "If you won't come with me, then I guess I'm bunking in my car, as well. I'll just bring it over here."

"You can't do that," Chelsea said. "That's…extreme and—"

"It's the only thing I can do," he said, his irritation climbing even higher. "You get to decide what you're doing, and I get to decide what I'm doing. No use arguing."

She stared at him and he stared right back, neither speaking. Finally, she nodded and started to roll up her window. He'd taken three full steps when she said, "Wait. Just…wait."

Dylan paused, pivoted and leveraged his hands on his hips. "Waiting."

"Can you promise… You're not an ax murderer or something, are you?"

"No," he said, choosing not to point out the obvious—most ax murderers didn't go around warning their would-be victims of their intent. "I find axes rather—" he smiled, more in an effort to put her at ease than from any sense of amusement "—unwieldy as a rule."

Her eyes widened in shock and she made a half squeal sort of a noise. No more than a second later, she blinked and her lips twitched in an almost grin. Good sign, that. "I see," she said. "So I don't have to worry that you're an ax murderer?"

"Nope," he said, straight-faced. "I'd rather put my victims in a car with no running heat on a cold, blustery night and wait for them to freeze to death. Far less bloody that way."

"Less bloody, sure, but not exactly the most expedient plan." She laughed, but it sounded forced to Dylan's ears. Nervous, too. "I believe you're not an ax murderer, but if I were to accept your offer of help…" Sighing, she glanced over her shoulder at her sleeping son. "Are you expecting anything in return? That is, anything *from me* in return?"

Oh, Lord. He should've seen that question coming. Every ounce of irritation fled. He no longer speculated on why Chelsea hadn't planned ahead well enough to have a place to sleep or what had happened to cause her job to fall through. All he saw was a desperate woman who was petrified she'd have to pay too high a price to keep her son warm.

It was, Dylan realized, far too easy to imagine Haley in such a position, even though she didn't yet have any children. And it was far too terrifying to consider if a different sort of man had offered his assistance. "All I'm expecting," he said, meeting Chelsea's gaze with his own and hoping she'd see his sincerity, "is to feel relief I didn't leave you and Henry out here on your own. That's it. That's all there is to this. I swear."

He could damn near see the debate raging inside her head, but in the end, she closed her eyes and released another sigh. "Whatever it takes," she muttered to herself. Then, with eyes wide-open and focused on him, she nodded. "I'll take you up on your offer, and I'm grateful and appreciative, but—" now she narrowed those gorgeous eyes of hers and the tempo of her speech hardened "—I will warn you that if you try anything at all, I do *not* find axes too unwieldy. I am, in fact, comfortable with a wide array of weapons. Quite comfortable."

Meaning she'd kick his butt from here to Denver if he crossed a line. Well, no worries there. He wasn't that type of man. Never had been, never would be.

But he couldn't continue to deny his attraction toward her, either. He'd recognized her vulnerability early on, so it wasn't that alone. Nor was it solely the tough attitude she'd just displayed. Nope, it was the mix of the two that yanked at his heart.

Nah. More appropriate to call that specific recipe in a woman his Achilles' heel. A combination of traits in the opposite sex that tended to shove his common sense out the window in lieu of more basic, emotional responses. The need to protect, defend, take care of.

Once, so long ago now that it was almost difficult to remember his younger self, he'd married a woman with that same deadly blend of helplessness coated by an edge of steel. For a while, he'd been mesmerized by Elise's wants and needs and his own desire to protect. He'd fallen for every sob, every shaky breath, every whispered devotion without ever second-guessing her intent. She'd been good. So damn good he hadn't seen her betrayal coming.

But she'd set her sights on a different type of life than the one she was born into, so she'd used him as a...well, a stepping stone. When something better came along, she'd trounced his heart into smithereens and run off with another man. Pregnant, to boot. Not with his child, as he'd made damn sure of that before signing the divorce decree.

But yeah, for Elise, he'd been nothing more than a stop-gap. It still hurt, realizing that was all he'd meant to her.

He'd loved and trusted Elise. Her deceptions had left him scarred and vigilant. Smarter, though, too. Truth was, he couldn't blame Elise for his own stupidity. There had been signs, he was sure, of her manipulations. If he'd paid more attention, he would've recognized those signs, and in doing so, saved himself from a world of pain and humiliation.

So, no. Dylan would never again allow himself to be taken for a ride by a tough-as-nails damsel in distress. No matter how attractive or appealing that woman might be.

He gave himself a mental shake and focused on Chelsea, who was still watching him with cautious eyes and a firm, unyielding mouth. Vulnerable and tough and... scared.

Yep, his Achilles' heel.

"Got it," he said, his tone abrupt and cool. "You're an ace with weaponry of all kinds. Now, if you're done with the warnings, let's get the two of you inside where it's warm. We'll get your car towed tomorrow and see about getting it fixed."

He thought for a second she was going to present a whole new slew of arguments. But then she unlocked her door and stepped out. While Chelsea gathered her son, he grabbed the overnight bags she pointed to, along with a patched-up stuffed bear that had seen better days.

And when Henry opened his eyes and asked his mother if they'd found their new fresh start, Dylan's heart about broke in two. But that feeling would lead him straight into disaster, so he shored up his defenses and promised to keep both mother and son at a distance.

A modest enough promise to stick to for one night.

Helping Chelsea and her son was the right thing to do. No more, no less. Tomorrow, he expected she'd be on her way back to wherever she'd come from. This pull he felt toward her wouldn't have the opportunity to grow or become problematic.

It would simply disappear.

Chapter Three

Panic and nausea roiled in Chelsea's stomach as she followed Dylan through the parking lot toward the back of the restaurant. She clutched Henry's hand tighter—he'd woken the second she'd attempted to lift him into her arms and had insisted on walking—and wished she weren't so afraid. What type of woman trusted a man's word when she didn't even know the man?

Well, she supposed, the type of woman who had run out of options. A sad, pitiful, terrifying description that now fit her perfectly.

She'd called each of the hotels Dylan had circled, plus a couple more for good measure. They were all cheap, but not cheap enough, and even then, none of them had any vacancies until tomorrow night. When the fight broke out, she'd decided it was best to leave, so she'd returned to the table and told Henry they were going to try something different that night by camping in their car. And yes, she'd made the prospect sound fun and adventurous.

Her darling, sweet boy didn't put up a fuss or ask too many questions. Rather, he nodded and smiled and asked—again—if he could have a root beer before they left. Of course, she'd expected he'd react well. That was her kid. He just sort of went with the flow—though the way life had treated them since his birth almost demanded such a disposition. Nothing had gone easy.

Disowned by her parents, which honestly had been more of a blessing than a curse, abandoned by Henry's father and left to her own devices to figure out all the messy details. Where to live. Where to work. Whom to trust. How to be the mother that Henry deserved.

And every damn time she thought she'd made a little progress, something would go wrong. Her apartment building had caught on fire. The best job she'd ever had, which wasn't saying much, had been eliminated. Her purse was stolen. Her car broke down.

One thing after another. She'd barely recovered from one disaster when a new one would occur. It was as if fate had decided that nothing—meaning not *one* thing—would ever go as planned. So, she supposed, not only had Henry learned to go with the flow, but she had, as well.

But this? Accepting help from a strange man and trusting he wasn't going to turn into a monster the second he had them alone was a new, frightening obstacle. Her gut told her he was safe and trustworthy, but her brain insisted she had just made a gigantic mistake.

So as they trudged along, she considered what she had in her purse that could be, if needed, used as a weapon. Her keys, maybe. If she could get them spread through her fingers just right fast enough. There was the minibottle of hair spray. Might work well enough if she could get the spray to hit his eyes, to blind him momentarily. Give her a few seconds to…what? Run?

She tried to imagine running with Henry at her side

or in her arms and knew they wouldn't get very far. Her keys, then. She'd use the hair spray to gain enough minutes to get to her keys, which she'd then use to protect herself and her son. After that, she didn't know, but stupid or not, she felt considerably better having any sort of a plan.

"My parents used to keep an apartment upstairs," Dylan was saying as they approached the back door of the restaurant. "All of us kids lived there at one time or another. Now it's more of a space for family meetings, but there are sofas and blankets, and it's warm."

"Sounds considerably better than the car," she said, her thoughts still focused on defense. And whether she fell into the cautious-but-smart category or the too-stupid-to-live one. She hoped the former. The too-stupid-to-live women always ended up dead in the movies. "I'm sure it's fine."

They stepped inside, and Chelsea dropped Henry's hand to fish through her purse. The second she found the hair-spray bottle, she pulled her son close to her side and, at the same time, put a little more breathing distance between them and Dylan. Just in case.

"Back so soon? I told you that Gavin is on his way, big brother, so there's no reason to… Oh!" The waitress who'd served them earlier rounded the corner, stopping short when she saw Chelsea and Henry. "I see we have company," she said. "Let me guess…car problems?"

"Hey, Haley. And yup, you guessed right," Dylan said. "This is Chelsea and Henry, and their car doesn't seem to like the cold weather all that much. They…ah…didn't have anywhere to stay, so I figured they could sleep upstairs. Just for tonight."

Relief filtered in, wiping out most of Chelsea's nerves. Someone else was here, and that made all of this seem much more normal. She loosened her hold on Henry.

"Okay," Haley said, as if such an occurrence happened on a regular basis. And hey, as far as Chelsea knew, strangers often slept upstairs. Then the woman knelt in front of Henry. "Hello there," she said. "Remember me? I brought you your hamburger and fries for dinner."

"'Course I remember. You forgot the dip," Henry said. "But you got it after I told you."

Haley laughed. "That's right." A series of raps on the door had her straightening into a stand. "That would be Gavin," she said to Dylan. "Are you all set, or...?"

"We're good. Go home and get some sleep."

"I think I will." Haley waved at Chelsea and Henry before giving Dylan a quick hug. "See you all tomorrow," she said, unlocking and opening the door. "Sleep tight and don't—"

"Let the bedbugs bite!" Henry said, finishing Haley's sentence. "Mommy says that all the time, except she tells me to let the love bugs bite." He scowled. "I don't want any bug bites!"

"Aw, that's cute," Haley said with another laugh. "Well, then, just sleep tight."

Dylan locked the door behind his sister and Chelsea's former apprehension returned. Not as strong, but still potent. Sensible, she knew, even with the normalcy of the exchange between Dylan and Haley. Better to be on guard and prepared than oblivious and taken by surprise.

"Anyone need anything before we head upstairs?" Dylan asked.

"It's too late for soda," Chelsea said to Henry, anticipating his response. "If you're thirsty, you can have water."

"Can I have a root beer tomorrow with lunch?" Henry asked. "You won't let me have soda for breakfast, so I won't ask for that."

"Yes, Henry," she said, too tired and nervous to worry about tomorrow.

"He really likes root beer, I take it?" Dylan didn't wait

for a reply, just gestured toward a door on the other side of the kitchen. "Let's go on up and get you settled."

"I like this new fresh start, Mommy," Henry said, following Dylan without a second's hesitation. "The other house was nice, but this one is better. It has the biggest kitchen I've ever seen and they have burgers and fries and real live fights! Pow, pow!"

"We left right after that fight started," Chelsea explained as they climbed a narrow flight of stairs, pretending with everything she had that she was as comfortable as Dylan seemed. "And he was a little bummed to miss the excitement."

"You know, Henry," Dylan said, opening the door at the top of the stairs. He reached in and flipped on the lights. "Fights might seem exciting, but they're dangerous and not the best way to settle a disagreement. Typically, anyway. So you didn't miss much."

"To him, it was noisy and fun." Wrong, probably, but Chelsea felt the need to defend Henry's enthusiasm. "He's just a child and hasn't yet connected fights with violence, because he has had zero exposure to violence. Which is how it should be."

"Yup, that is exactly how it should be. I wasn't condemning his view, just pointing out a different one. That's all." Herding them into the brightly lit room, Dylan said, "When I was a kid, me and my brothers were almost always in some sort of a skirmish. It's natural."

"Right. I just… I thought you were… Never mind."

"You thought I was remarking on your parenting skills or something along those lines?"

"I don't know. Maybe." To change the subject, she asked, "You said your brothers, as in plural? How many? Older or younger?"

"Two. One older, one younger."

She waited for additional details, but he didn't offer

any. Disappointed, though she couldn't put into words why, she said, "I have one sister. Younger."

"That's good. Family is important."

"Depends on the family," she said, thinking of her upbringing. Her father's near-constant state of displeasure, with just about everything, really, but most often focused on Chelsea. Her mother's passive disregard or worse, when she chimed in with her own cruel words in an effort to appease her husband rather than standing up for her kids. And Chelsea's inability to succeed in their eyes, despite her many attempts. "Some families aren't very family-like."

Dylan gave her a question-filled look but didn't comment. That was fine. She didn't talk about her family with anyone. Not the details, at any rate. Her response had been made out of nervousness and a need to keep the silence at bay.

"We're sleeping here?" Henry spun in a circle, taking in the space. "There aren't any beds! Mommy, we could build a fort under the table. Like an inside tent!"

Chuckling, Dylan said, "This used to be the living room. Now it's a meeting space." He deposited the overnight bags and Teddy on the large rectangular table before nodding toward the adjoining kitchenette. "There should be water bottles in the fridge, and you'll probably find some snacks in the cupboard. Nothing fancy, but my family likes to eat."

"I'm sure we'll be fine," Chelsea said. "And really, this is so nice—"

"Can we make a fort?" Henry ran over to the table and pulled out one of the chairs. "Like that time we didn't have any beds? Remember, Mommy?"

Heat flooded her face. Of course she remembered. It had been after the fire, and most of what they'd had was too smoke damaged to keep. Months had passed before she'd replaced even half of the items they'd lost. She'd never replaced her bed, but Henry's she had.

And even that awful set of circumstances had been better than this.

"Yes, Henry, I remember. But I don't know about building a fort. This isn't—"

"No reason to, not that forts aren't fun. But that room over there," Dylan said, "used to be the bedroom. We've turned it into a break room of sorts. There's a couple of sofas that you two can sleep on, and there should be plenty of blankets and a few pillows in the closet. You'll have privacy. Bathroom is back there, as well. Make yourself at home."

"I'm sure we'll be fine," Chelsea repeated. "This is nice of you. More than nice."

"Nice is nice. I'm not sure what being more than nice entails." Dylan shook his head, frustration appearing in the rigid set of his shoulders. "I'm not doing anything that any other decent person wouldn't."

"I don't have that experience," she said. "Regardless, it's kind and you could've walked away to begin with. You didn't. You came over to see what the problem was. That alone is more than I'm accustomed to, and I—" Snapping her mouth shut, irritated she'd given even that much of her life away, she finished with "Thank you. Because of you, we're not sleeping in the car."

Compassion and concern glittered in Dylan's eyes, darkening them into a smoky green. But when he spoke, she didn't hear either. What she heard was sharp annoyance. "Offering help when someone is in need is the decent thing to do, especially when it's an easy fix. This is an easy fix for your dilemma. Most of the folks I know would do the same. If you don't know people like that, then I'd say you're hanging with the wrong crowd."

Whoa. What had riled him up so much? "That isn't

what I meant," she said in a rush. "I'm saying thank you for being so decent. Why can't you accept a simple thank-you?"

"Stop being mad," Henry said in a wobbly, uncertain voice. "I don't like it."

"Oh, honey, we're not mad. We're just talking. Promise!" Chelsea wrapped her arm around her son's shoulders and pulled him close for a hug. When she let go, she said, "Everyone is tired, that's all. Nothing to worry about, sweetie."

"That's right. No one's mad," Dylan said quickly in a warmer tone. "As your mom said, we're tired. It's late and we've all had a long day. Me with work and you two with driving."

"Exactly." Chelsea picked up the bags from the table and Henry's stuffed animal—hers, actually, from her childhood. A gift from Sophia. "Let's say good-night and get some sleep."

"Good night," Henry said, tugging on Dylan's shirt so he was forced to look down at him. "And thank you for not letting us camp in our car. It wasn't as fun as I thought. And for making Mommy not cry anymore. I don't like it when she cries."

Emotion clogged Chelsea's throat. She hadn't realized Henry had heard her crying.

Dylan blinked once, twice. "I don't like it when my mom cries, either. So you're welcome, Henry. I'm glad I can help. And don't give up on camping just yet. It can be fun when the weather is nice and you have a warm sleeping bag and a campfire to roast marshmallows."

"That would be fun," Henry said, rubbing his eyes. "Maybe you can take me and Mommy camping sometime? I don't think she'd know how to make a campfire."

"Oh, I think I could figure it out," Chelsea said, feeling the very real need for solitude. To think. To rest. To gather her bearings. She looked at Dylan and moved her lips into some semblance of a smile. "Thank you," she said, her voice firm. "But I can take it from here."

She led Henry in the direction of the room Dylan had said they could sleep in, and just as she opened the door, she heard him say, "You're welcome, Chelsea."

And strangely, even with the turmoil of the day and her extreme unease at accepting help from anyone, let alone a man she'd only just met, the sound of Dylan's voice in that second added a level of comfort, of safety, into her swirling emotions. There was something about him that tugged at her sensibilities, made her want to lean into him and…just let him take care of all the messy details. And how screwed up was that?

She was fine on her own. Well, mostly fine.

The last thing she needed in her complicated life was another complication. Even so, as she made up the sofas with the blankets and pillows she found in the closet, she remembered her earlier wish—to have allowed just one trustworthy person into her life—and she couldn't help but wonder if she let her guard down enough, if maybe Dylan would prove to be that person.

Unlikely—because, as he'd so plainly said, he was only doing what any decent person would do—but it was a nice thought. Nice and…hopeful. And right now she'd take any bit of hope she could find. She'd wanted, had prayed, for a new fresh start to present itself.

Perhaps this night, her car's demise and trusting in Dylan's words and accepting his help—for tonight *only*—was the beginning of a better life. For her and for Henry. Perhaps.

If not, well, she'd gone down that road plenty. It was familiar, if not friendly, ground.

Yawning, Dylan attempted for what had to be the hundredth time to find a comfortable way to sleep while stretched out between two straight-backed, hard-as-a-rock meeting-table chairs. He carefully maneuvered his arm behind his head to function as a cushion and at the same time flexed his legs to try loosening his tight muscles.

Bad idea. The movement was enough to overturn the chair his feet rested on, and in three seconds flat, he'd toppled to the floor. He pulled himself to a sitting position and pressed his forehead against his knees. Nope. Using those chairs as a bed couldn't be done.

Not by him, at any rate.

If he'd had his wits about him, he'd have grabbed a blanket and a pillow before Chelsea and Henry had turned in for the night. Now their door was closed and he guessed—based on Chelsea's earlier concerns—locked tight. At this point, he'd be fortunate to grab a meager four hours of shut-eye, let alone the nine he'd originally hoped for.

Hell. Luck had nothing to do with it. Even if he somehow managed to contort his body in such a way to relax enough to fall asleep, thoughts of the woman and her child in the next room would keep him awake. Standing, he shoved the chairs back into their normal positions and went to the fridge for a bottle of water. He'd gone without sleep before—he'd get by.

Unscrewing the cap, he took a long swig and considered his options. Morning would come fast. He was supposed to clock in at the sporting-goods store by twelve, where he'd work until four. Then he'd stop by Reid and Daisy's place to check in on his sister-in-law and his four-month-old niece and nephew, Charlotte and Alexander.

Twins. Who would've guessed?

Not Reid. Apparently, the sight of two babies on the ultrasound monitor had thrown Dylan's typically stoic older brother into a state of near collapse. Or, as Daisy had explained, "His face turned white and he almost fainted in shock."

Hard to imagine, that. But Reid's job as a ski patroller, along with the help he provided the family's businesses, meant extralong, exhausting hours during the winter season. Since September, Dylan—well, all of the Fosters, really—had taken to dropping in on a daily basis. First to keep Daisy company—and appease Reid's concerns, which had grown at the same rate as the size of Daisy's stomach—in the last months of her pregnancy, and now to lend a hand. And Dylan enjoyed hanging with Daisy and helping with the babies.

Well, okay, he wasn't all that fond of spit-up. Or changing diapers. But the rest of it was good. Family, in Dylan's estimation, was all that really mattered.

After his stint there, he'd return to the pub by seven to tend the bar. Another long day awaited him, and this one he'd have to tackle with limited energy. Easier knowing it was the last crazy day of the season and that he'd then have more than enough hours to refuel.

Without thought, he tipped his head toward the room Chelsea and Henry slept in and mentally added them to his to-do list for the day. That car would have to be towed, and hopefully repaired, early enough so they could be on their way. They *had* to be on their way, quick-like, before he gave in to the impulse to fix not only her car, but her life.

Henry's words rang in Dylan's ears. *She'd cried.* And at some point they hadn't owned beds, so they'd slept in a fort. Of course, that could mean something as simple as they'd just moved and their furniture had yet to be delivered. Could mean that.

But he didn't think it did.

Closing his eyes, Dylan mentally replayed everything he'd seen and heard since Chelsea had first walked into Foster's. Her body language, her words—what she'd ad-

mitted to and what she hadn't, what he could only speculate on—the fear and desperation he'd recognized in her
expression and the bits of information that Henry had in-
advertently shared.

He'd already pieced together enough, even before finding her stranded in her car, to realize she was in a jam.
Until this minute, though, he'd categorized her current
predicament as a momentary spell of bad luck. Most people had family and friends to rely on in such moments, to
get them through to better days. While he hadn't given
it a whole lot of thought, somewhere in his brain he'd
assumed she had the same and that when she returned
home—wherever home was—she'd have that support.
But dammit, his gut told him that wasn't the case.

And if so, what was he to do about that?

The sound of a door opening, followed by a quick
gasp of surprise, interrupted his thought process. When
he looked, he saw the woman herself, plastered against
the door frame, wearing a long pink T-shirt and loose,
candy-cane-striped pajama bottoms. Tension tightened
her mouth, and all he wanted to do was make her smile.

"It occurs to me," he said with what he hoped was
a friendly, not-threatening-at-all tenor, "that I've yet to
learn your last name. You know mine, but in case you
forgot, it's Foster."

"Oh. Um...our last name is Bell," she said, her voice
holding that husky, barely awake quality. Also, though, a
thread of wariness. "Chelsea and Henry Bell."

"Nice to officially meet you, Chelsea Bell," Dylan said,
curious if a Mr. Bell existed somewhere or if Chelsea had
simply never married and Henry had her name. Dammit.
He shouldn't care. "Something wake you or were you
looking for me?"

"I... No, not looking for you. I thought I'd get a bottle
of water, but I didn't expect to see you up here. I guess I

thought you'd go downstairs or—" She broke off, bit her bottom lip. "Dumb assumption to have. Why would you leave us alone when I could be a thief or—"

"An ax murderer?" Dylan asked in dry humor. "Sorry, but I don't believe we have even one ax on the premises. And if you're a thief, you can't be that great at your job."

"Is that so? What makes you say that?"

"Let's start with the look of that car out there."

"Perhaps I'm an excellent thief and my car is a…um… cover." A soft, sleepy smile appeared. And she went from cute to beautiful. Breathtakingly so. "To hide my true, nefarious intent and the fact that I have oodles of diamonds and gold nuggets hidden away in the trunk."

"Diamonds and gold nuggets? Good to know. We won't just fix your car tomorrow, we'll buy you a new one. Something more appropriate for a nefarious diamond-and-gold-nugget thief."

"I…" Pushing away from the door frame, she approached the kitchenette. "If I can't afford a hotel room, I certainly can't afford whatever repairs that car needs. I was thinking of trying to sell it to a junkyard. Maybe I can get a couple hundred bucks."

"I already guessed you didn't have the finances for the tow or the repairs, so I thought I'd front you the money. It's no trouble." Dylan swallowed another gulp of water, curious as to what type of damsel in distress she actually was. Would she put up all sorts of arguments before giving in and accepting his help? Or would she be like Elise and not even bother with the pretense, smile sweetly and thank him for his kindness? Or would she have an entirely different type of reaction? "You can pay me back after you get home and settled. There isn't any rush."

She stopped her forward motion and frowned. Shook her head as if she had water stuck in her ears after a long dip in the pool. "What did you just say?"

Okay, then. A different type of reaction. He repeated his words, verbatim. And waited with interest to see what road she'd take them down next.

"Thank you, but no," she said. Her eyes, her voice—everything about her—were cool and crisp and matter-of-fact. He'd irritated her? Yup, that he had, and his interest increased. Tenfold. "The truth is, I have more use of a couple hundred bucks in my wallet than I do with that car and owing you who knows how much money. So, again, thank you but no."

She meant her words. And that told Dylan a hell of a lot about her character. More, probably, than she'd like him to know. Still didn't mean he trusted her or wanted her to stick around. Only once had a woman affected him in as strong and intense a fashion as this woman. He'd fallen for Elise, hard. And look where that path had taken him?

"That's fine," he said, opening the fridge and tossing her a bottle of water. She caught it easily. "I'll help you with that in the morning and, once you have the cash, drive you over to the bus station. If I run out of time, someone in my family will be happy to help."

"Why, you're just full of helpful suggestions, aren't you?"

"Trying, I guess," he said, watching her carefully. She wasn't just irritated, she was…well, fuming would be the right description. "Something wrong with that?"

"No." She sucked in a large breath, held it and then let it out with a loud whoosh of air. "Yes, actually. Yes, there is something wrong with that."

"Care to explain?"

"Just that…you don't know me and I don't know you. It isn't your call what I do next," she said, her words coming at a fast clip, as if she was afraid common sense would reel them back in. "I am very appreciative of your assistance tonight, but when morning comes, I'll go about my business and leave you to yours. So, no, I won't be requiring a ride to the bus station from you or your family. I don't even *need* to go to the bus station."

Ah, hell. "You're planning on staying, then?"

"I'm planning on staying," she confirmed, losing her steam. She stared at her toes—which were painted a dark shade of purple—and exhaled, brought her gaze back to his. "I told Henry this was our fresh start at a brand-new life, and I am not going to disappoint him again."

And double hell.

"You don't have a job," he said, stating the obvious. "Or a place to live."

"I'll find both. And until I do—" she lifted her chin in stubborn hope "—I'll find one of those cheap motels and pray I get enough from selling the Malibu to see us through."

Before he could stop himself, before his logic kicked in and squelched that damn desire to protect, defend and take care of, he heard himself saying, "If you're dead and determined to stay, we'll figure out something better than a cheap motel. And once I talk to my family, we might be able to scrounge up some work. On a temporary basis, that is."

Dark blue eyes blinked in surprise and emotion. *Sappy* emotion. She looked away, off to his left, and a tremble coursed through her body. "I've never met a man like you, but as shockingly kind as your offer is, this time I'll have to say no."

"You said no about sleeping here and changed your mind."

"I did. Because of Henry."

"Who is still in the picture, unless he jumped out the window and ran away?"

She looked at him then, all soft and vulnerable and… beautiful. It took every ounce of willpower not to walk the few inches between them, pull her into his arms and promise her that everything would be fine. Better than fine. That she didn't have to worry.

Fortunately, he ignored that instinct and waited her out.

"I can take care of my son," she said. "I have since the day he was born, without anyone swooping in to help or fix my problems."

And wasn't that a damn shame? He shook off the thought and shrugged. "Not swooping," he said. "Just extending a hand, but as you said, it's your call."

"That's right. And…and I have a plan."

He didn't state the numerous flaws her plan held. Such as, even if she located employment right off the bat, she wouldn't receive an actual paycheck for two weeks. Maybe longer. And the cheapest not-a-dump motel in town that he knew of—even with the less expensive off-season rates that would start in a few days—hovered around the fifty-dollar-per-night range. Supposing she got five hundred dollars for her car, and he thought that was the most the junkyard paid, she'd only have enough funds for a week.

But he didn't point out any of these facts. Instead, he gave her a short nod and said, "You should get some sleep. Tomorrow will be a long day. For both of us."

Chelsea opened her mouth as if to say more, but closed it just as fast. Another visible tremble swept through her slender body before she disappeared behind the safety of her closed door. Dylan stood there and tried—oh, he tried—not to make her and her son his responsibility.

Because nothing had changed there, either. They weren't.

She was in a tough predicament, yes, but she had refused his help. That should be enough to allow him to walk away without feeling any residual guilt. He couldn't, though.

Just couldn't.

Swearing quietly, he finished off his water and tossed the empty bottle into the trash. He'd see what he could do about giving Chelsea and Henry Bell their new fresh start, but without her knowledge. And once they were adequately settled, he'd put both of them out of his head and wipe his hands of the whole ordeal.

Before his Foster DNA kicked in again and had him doing something even more insane. Like falling in love with both mother and son. Nope. That couldn't happen.

Wouldn't. Happen. No way in hell.

Chapter Four

The sound of a door thudding shut followed by short, quick footsteps scampering across the hardwood floor woke Dylan with nearly the same effectiveness as a shotgun blast. Well, to say he'd been fast asleep would be an overstatement. Fitfully dozing, perhaps.

Squinting open one eye, he saw Henry, who was clothed in the brightest fire-engine-red pajamas Dylan had ever seen, approach the minifridge. Assuming the boy would grab a bottle of water and return to the other room, Dylan closed his eyes and feigned sleep.

What had he gotten himself into? How in the hell was he going to create a brand-new fresh start for a vulnerable, stubborn woman and her feisty child?

It was a helluva lot. More than he'd originally realized when he'd arrived at the harebrained scheme a few short hours ago. Chelsea required a job, a place to live, child care for Henry and, unless the prior three were within walking distance of each other, reliable transportation until she could afford to buy another car.

Again, he considered the simplest action: leaving her to her own devices and going on his merry way as if they'd never met. And once again the tension in his gut told him—in no uncertain terms—that he couldn't. Nope, she was not his *logical* responsibility. That was fact. Yet fate had seen to it that she'd walked into his family's restaurant, that her car had broken down in their parking lot and that he'd been the Foster to find her.

Sensible didn't have a foothold in the equation.

Urgency to get started overtook his body's desire to sleep, but Henry hadn't yet returned to his mother. Once he did, Dylan would go downstairs and call the junkyard, see about getting someone over here within the next few hours. Then he'd check in with his family to see if they had any ideas, and if all went well, he'd soon have the beginnings of a plan in place.

The thought had no sooner crossed his mind when Dylan heard a door open and close, and then the telltale sounds of Henry all but running down the stairs to the restaurant's kitchen. Dammit all. What was that kid up to?

Sitting, Dylan wiped the grit from his eyes and contemplated his next move. The kid couldn't be more than four or five, tops, and the kitchen wasn't exactly childproofed.

He stood and followed Henry's trail, taking the stairs two at a time, thoughts of sharp knives and gas-burning stoves filling his heart with dread. When he entered the kitchen, he stopped and waited for his pulse to return to normal. The kid was standing in front of the commercial refrigerator, his sandy-brown hair spiked and mussed from sleep, with the door wide-open. He was staring at its contents so intently he seemed oblivious to Dylan's presence.

"Morning, Henry," he said. "Hungry, I take it?"

The boy startled, sending a tremor through his thin,

almost bony body. "You scared me! You shouldn't do that. Mommy says it's not nice to scare people."

"Sorry, kid. But you probably shouldn't be exploring on your own." At least, not in a room filled with an abundance of child-safety hazards. If Dylan hadn't been awake, *anything* could have happened. He shoved that thought far into the abyss—the boy was fine, after all—and asked, "Does your mom know you're down here, or is she still sleeping?"

"I told her and she said she'd get up in five minutes, but she didn't."

"Ah." And that, Dylan knew from his own childhood, was equivalent to receiving permission to go ahead and do as you pleased. "Well, I bet your mom is more tired than usual."

"Right, so I 'cided to let her sleep." Henry finally turned to look at Dylan. "She was sad last night. I thought if I made her breakfast, she'd smile. I like it when she smiles."

Unexpected emotion gathered in Dylan's throat. He swallowed it down, nodded and knelt in front of Henry. "That's a fine idea. Mind if I help? I'd like to see your mom smile, too."

"Don't know," Henry said, his tone solemn. "Do you cook good or bad?"

"Um. Neither, I guess. More like somewhere in between."

Narrowing his eyes in contemplation, the tyke tapped his chin with the practiced seriousness of a fifty-year-old business magnate in the middle of a high-stakes negotiation. "I guess it's okay if you help, but I'm in charge. It was my idea."

"True. Though, you do realize that being in charge is a big responsibility? Maybe we could agree to be partners?" Dylan ruffled Henry's hair. "What do you say?"

"I know what foods Mommy likes and what she doesn't like," Henry pointed out, expertly avoiding both of Dylan's questions. "Do you know what foods she likes?"

"Other than bread and coffee, nope."

"Then I should be in charge."

Sensing this conversation could continue ad nauseam unless someone gave in, Dylan took the fall. "All righty, then, you call the shots and I'll cook." Pleasure at winning gleamed in Henry's eyes, and Dylan forced back a chuckle. "Does you mom like eggs? Peanut-butter toast? Oatmeal? Or—"

"Nothing with peanut butter! She hates peanut butter because she's…she's—" Henry curled his bottom lip into his mouth as he searched for the correct word "—allergic! Gives her itchy bumps and makes her cough. She wouldn't smile then. So, no peanut butter."

Amused, Dylan nodded. He distinctly remembered Henry stating that his mother had eaten a peanut-butter sandwich for breakfast the prior day, so he doubted she was allergic. No sense in arguing with the guy in charge, though. "You're right. Coughing and itchy rashes don't typically make people smile. How does scrambled eggs and toast sound?"

"Okay, but not good enough." Henry stubbed his toe into the tile floor. "I want her to smile a lot. And be really happy. So something better."

"Something better, huh? What about—"

Before Dylan could finish his sentence, the back door to the kitchen opened, sending a blast of cold air into the room. His mother. Had to be. In all likelihood, Haley had already spread the news about his overnight guests. And no way, no how, would Margaret Foster set aside her curiosity or her concern until she'd deemed nothing was amiss.

Thank God, too. His mom could cook up a storm. Better yet, once she learned of Chelsea's unfortunate set of circumstances, she would be more than happy to help.

"Hi, Mom," Dylan said as he heard her soft-footed approach. "Perfect timing. We're trying to decide what to make for breakfast, and it's a tall order. We could use your input."

Margaret's concerned expression transformed into a cheerful smile the instant she realized a child was in attendance. She unbuttoned and removed her coat, which she hung on one of the wall hooks, saying, "Then it's a good thing I decided to come right over. What are we trying to accomplish with breakfast? Other than no more empty tummies, that is."

"We want to make my mommy smile," Henry said. "And I'm Henry. I'm four! And I slept upstairs last night because our car wouldn't turn on no more."

"It is so nice to meet you, Henry! I'm Margaret, Dylan's mom, and we'll come up with the perfect breakfast." Then, with a nod toward the still-open refrigerator door, she said, "Tell me, though, are you two trying to cool the kitchen or warm up the fridge?"

"Both, actually," Dylan said, moving out of his mother's way. "We were in the middle of conducting a science experiment on how fast temperatures can change. Isn't that right, Henry?"

"Nope, that isn't right." He cast those innocent eyes of his on Margaret and, with an impish grin, said, "I was looking for food, but then he asked me a bunch of questions. I forgot about the door and he didn't tell me to close it. He's the grown-up, though, so it's his fault."

"Hey! You're going to get me in trouble!" In a completely spontaneous movement, Dylan picked up Henry and swung him around in the air. Little-boy giggles along with Margaret's surprised laughter poured into the room, and Dylan's heart...well, it friggin' soared.

Really wasn't a better way to phrase the sensation.

When he set Henry safely on the floor, he said, "I'm not so grown-up that my mom can't ground me…or worse. She might look and act all nice and sweet, but she's tough."

Margaret sniffed, reached behind them to shut the refrigerator door. "Had to be tough, raising boys like you and your brothers. Trouble, all three of you."

"And Haley was a princess?"

"Haley was about the same trouble as the three of you combined, and yes, she is and always has been the princess of the family. But that," Margaret said with a pointed look at Dylan, "wasn't due to me or your father. That girl was spoiled rotten by you and your brothers."

Yeah, well, true enough. Haley's entrance into the Foster family had been met with spectacular awe, enormous love and fierce loyalty from each of the Foster brothers. She was theirs to care for, to protect, to teach and to guide. Reid, Dylan and Cole had taken their role as her big brothers to heart. They still did. Probably always would.

It was, Dylan realized with some shock, a type of affection not so different from what he'd just experienced with Henry in his arms, hearing his high-pitched, happy-as-all-get-out giggles. But that was an emotion typically only connected with family.

Certainly *not* with strangers.

Loud warning bells went off in Dylan's head, which he flat-out ignored. Henry was a cute kid, and really, who didn't enjoy the sound of a child's laugh? Dylan closed his eyes and pushed out a breath. He'd shared a fun moment with Henry. That was it.

"Are you feeling okay?" Suddenly, his mother's cool palm was pressed tight against his forehead. "No fever, but you're paler than normal."

"I'm fine." Dylan opened his eyes and smiled. "Promise. Just tired."

"Hmm. If you say so."

"I do." Though he'd be better once he got everything back on track. He'd start with the junkyard. "I need to make a quick phone call. Can you help Henry with breakfast?"

"Of course." Margaret retreated a few inches and gave him another once-over before focusing on Henry. "Pancakes or waffles? Which do you think is the most smileworthy?"

"Waffles!" Henry said without a second's hesitation. "With blueberries and syrup and lots and lots of whippy cream and bacon. I love... I mean, Mommy loves bacon!"

"Excellent choices, but maybe we'll go light on the whippy cream," Margaret said, pulling on an apron and tying the straps around her waist. "Let's grab a chair and move it to the sink, and you can be a big help by cleaning the blueberries. I'll show you how."

Dylan made his way toward the main restaurant and bar area, waiting until the last possible second before exiting the kitchen to say, "I should only be a few minutes. And later this morning, if we can get everyone over here, I'd like to set up a family meeting."

"It's already set," Margaret said, her voice a tad too bubbly for Dylan's peace of mind. "Everyone will be here shortly, so don't go running off anywhere."

Her statement made him pause. "Why'd you call everyone so fast?"

"It isn't every day that you invite perfect strangers to stay the night, now, is it? Seemed unusual enough to merit a discussion. Apparently, I was correct."

"Right. Well...okay, then. Thanks." With that, he left the kitchen and approached the bar, his brain on high alert. His mother's intuition was an unexplainable phenomenon that, at times, drove him and the rest of his siblings nuts. She knew her kids well.

If she tuned in to his—what should he call it? Interest?—in Chelsea, she wouldn't leave well enough alone. She would butt into not only his business—in her own sweet, graceful and kind way, of course—but Chelsea's, as well. If his brothers and sister sensed the same, his predictable and simple life would cease to exist.

They had each behaved more than a little crazily when it came to winning over their respective significant others. Between the three of them, there had been one outlandish scheme after another. Cole's pretend, completely fictionalized girlfriend to make Rachel jealous. Haley's sneaky maneuvers to capture Gavin's attention. And Reid…well, he'd gone all out and planned an entire wedding when Daisy hadn't even agreed to marry him.

Well, he'd make darn sure there wasn't anything for his family to sense. His life was great just the way it was, and he didn't see why that had to change.

If, for some ridiculous reason, when all was said and done, his *interest* in Chelsea didn't abate, what then? Dylan's heart rammed hard in his chest and sweat beaded on the back of his neck. He didn't know. Didn't want to know, either.

He simply wouldn't go there again. Preferably with anyone, but absolutely not with a woman who could tie him into such tight knots so early in the game.

Later that morning, Chelsea stood outside in the cold bite of the wind and tried her best to mask her disappointment when the man from the junkyard offered her $350 for the Malibu. She'd hoped to get closer to five hundred, but really, any additional cash in her pocket gave her options that her broken-down, expensive-to-repair car did not.

Fact, yes, but losing the Malibu still stung.

Blinking back tears, she accepted the money the man counted into the palm of her hand. Now she and Henry were left with nothing but their clothes and the sparse personal belongings they'd brought with them. Some toys and books for Henry and a few—very few—pieces of memorabilia that held special meaning for Chelsea. Her son's baby blanket and the sleeper he'd worn home from the hospital, a couple of photo albums and, finally, her grandmother Sophia's recipe cards. The rest had been tossed or given to charity.

Earlier, after finding Henry preparing breakfast with Dylan's mother, Chelsea and Dylan had brought the boxes and suitcases and Henry's booster seat into the restaurant for safekeeping. Dylan had shared what had transpired that morning, and she had no memory of Henry waking her, so again, she was struck with that strange mix of gratitude and fear.

Gratitude that Dylan had heard Henry and had watched over him—heck, he and Margaret were watching him now while Chelsea dealt with this—and fear of what might have happened if he hadn't. Truth was, she hadn't slept that soundly in a very long time. Odd that she had relaxed enough to get any sleep, let alone in a new place with an unpredictable future facing her.

Even sharing breakfast with Dylan and his mother hadn't been too awkward. Other than a few questions regarding Chelsea's car, Margaret had kept the conversation to simple topics that involved Henry. Did he have a favorite toy? Had he learned the alphabet yet? Since he had, he then—naturally—had to prove so by reciting the letters. Not once, but twice.

Up until this very minute, Chelsea's first morning in Steamboat Springs had gone as well as it possibly could. But selling her car was more difficult than she'd thought. Sighing, she stepped backward and watched as the man readied the vehicle to be towed. Failure, strong and consuming, slammed onto her shoulders. Where would she and her son sleep tonight? How many days or weeks or months would it take her to get them back on their feet?

Chelsea drew in a breath to steady herself and watched as the Malibu was hauled away. She waited until the truck and the car were completely out of sight before allowing herself one minute to feel the full weight of her emotions. Better here, alone, than inside and in front of Henry, who remained blissfully unaware of the shaky ground they now stood on.

Yesterday had been awful. And okay, she'd had other awful days and bounced back, but this felt scarier than anything they'd yet experienced. She didn't have a home. Oh, God. *Her son* didn't have a home. He didn't have a bedroom or a bed or a place to store his books or toys. He didn't have… *Stop.*

She'd had those things as a child, and she'd still been miserable. So, no, Henry might not have a bedroom or a bed right now, but he had her. And come hell or high water, she wouldn't let him down. Straightening her spine—literally and figuratively—Chelsea wiped her eyes, shoved her fear and failure and panic into a corner, and headed for the restaurant.

Yesterday was over. Today would be better.

His family had shown up at the perfect time and for reasons unknown to him entered through the front of the restaurant. Haley, after learning the basic rundown from Dylan while their mother kept Henry occupied, had then taken the boy to the other room so he could talk to everyone else. Fortunately, he hadn't had to say much to get them on board.

The simple fact of keeping a mother and her young child off the streets had been more than enough, and a loose plan had been formed. *Very* loose and fairly flimsy, as far as plans went. Details still needed to be filled in and firmed, but it was better than nothing.

"Okay, she's on her way back," Dylan said, standing near the window.

"None of this might pan out," Cole said. "I'm not entirely positive that Dee's Deli even has an open position, and I have no idea where Chelsea and Henry might stay other than here or at a hotel. And this seems rushed, even to me. More time would be helpful."

"Yup, it would. But we don't have more time, and she won't agree to stay here another night." Dylan kept his eyes on Chelsea as she trekked through the parking lot. "A job comes first—the rest can follow. Reid? How fast can you find out if your pediatrician's office is still hiring?"

"I'll call Daisy when we're done and see if she knows," Reid said. "Cole's right, though. A little more time would go a long way. To get to know Chelsea, for one thing. Easier to help her find a job if I can give her a personal recommendation."

"She's a good person and she needs a job. So, I don't know, do it for me."

"And you know she's a good person how?" the patriarch of the family, Paul, asked. "Don't get me wrong, son, we should do what is reasonable, but you've only known this woman for a few hours. Not hardly long enough to ask your brothers to put their word on the line."

Frustrated, though unsure why—his father's assessment matched his own brand of logic, after all—Dylan faced his family. Cole and Reid were standing near the door to the bar area, while his parents were at the table. "Because I… It's one of those things, Dad. I just know. I'm supposed to do this." Then, looking at his mother, he said, "You met her. What do you think?"

"I like her," she said. "She seems lost right now, but perfectly sane and capable. And I'm pleased that you feel so strongly about helping her, which we will. But really, all we have to do is point her in the right direction. If the deli or the doctor's office is hiring, take her to those places. Chelsea will either have the experience to merit an interview or she won't."

Yet again, the logic was sound, but Dylan's frustration didn't ease. That woman—Chelsea Bell—was getting to him, both her and her child, and he wanted to do more than merely send them in the right direction and *hope* they were okay. He wanted them to be set.

But okay, a ridiculous way to feel. Especially so fast.

"Right. That's all I meant." Another quick look out the window showed that Chelsea was nearing the door. "Why don't you guys check in on Haley and Henry? Once I warn Chelsea you're all here, I'll bring her in for introductions."

"You seem tense, Dylan," Cole said, barely hiding his grin. "Makes me wonder if there's something else we should know before meeting Chelsea?"

Cripes. "Like what? I have a busy day. I'm supposed to be at the sporting-goods store by twelve and at Reid's by four-thirty. I'm juggling my responsibilities with trying to help Chelsea, and time is running short. That's it."

"The store will manage without you today," Cole said. "Do what you need to do."

"And if you can't be at my place this afternoon, Daisy will understand," Reid said without hesitation. "But something seems to be bothering you. Worries me, Dylan, since the way you're behaving now is similar to when you—"

"Stop. Please," Dylan said before Reid uttered Elise's name. His mother's intuition seemed to be spreading, and that was not a good sign. "I don't want to add to Chelsea's discomfort by having her walk into a room filled with strangers. So, vamoose already, okay?"

Paul, who'd watched the back-and-forth with a fair amount of interest, stood. "Move it," he said to Reid and

Cole. "No sense in arguing. We've agreed to help, and that's that. Whatever else you want to know, you can ask later."

Clamping his jaw shut, as if physically restraining himself from saying more, Reid nodded and exited the room, with Cole and their parents right behind him.

Three seconds later, Chelsea walked in.

Chapter Five

"**Y**ou okay?" Dylan asked the instant the door closed behind Chelsea. She turned, and there he was, strong and tall and far too appealing for a man she'd only just met. He smiled and butterflies dipped and bobbed in her stomach, adding to her nerves. "That had to be tough, selling your car. Brave, too, though. I'm sorry you had to make such a choice."

"Brave? Not hardly. It was the right choice."

"Just because something is right doesn't mean it's easy." He leaned against the wall, his arms angled over his chest, and looked her straight in the eyes. It was disconcerting. And more than a little intense. "You can argue if you want, but it won't change my mind."

Blinking to break the contact, she said, "Then I'll change the subject. Thank you for watching Henry. I hope he behaved and didn't cause too much trouble."

"Nah. He wasn't any trouble at all." Dylan nodded toward the main area of the restaurant. "My family is here, and Haley sort of fell under your son's spell. She wants to spend the day with him, thought she'd take him to her place. If you're okay with the idea, naturally, but she—"

"Wait. Just wait a minute," Chelsea interjected, taken off guard. "Why would your sister want to babysit a kid she barely knows? That seems odd."

"Not odd at all. Haley loves kids. In fact," Dylan said with a shrug, "she and her fiancé run a camp for foster children. The last group of boys left a week ago and the next won't be here until a little closer to summer. I think the place feels empty to her now."

"I see." She tried to gather her thoughts, tried to put her finger on what bothered her the most about this offer, and the best she came up with was "While that must be terrific for the kids, having a camp like that, Henry isn't a foster child. He also isn't Haley's responsibility. So, I'm guessing you asked her to babysit, and the only reason—"

"Whoa," Dylan said, holding up a hand. "Stop for a second and take a breath." She pressed her lips together and waited, but tapped her toe to show her impatience. "Did I say that Henry was a foster child or that I believe he is Haley's responsibility?"

"No. But you seem to think that I'm the sort of mother who will pawn her child off on a stranger, and that's not the type of parent I am." Irritation darkened her voice. She had *always* seen to Henry's welfare, which was why she had to get out of here. A job was not going to miraculously fall into her hands. "I take care of my son."

"If I somehow implied you didn't, I apologize." Again, Dylan's gaze hit her head-on. Again, her stomach dipped and bobbed. "But why are you so defensive? Are you in some type of trouble, Chelsea? Is someone, like Henry's father, looking for you? If so, maybe I can—"

"What? Help?" Forget irritation. True-blue anger took center stage. Still, she kept her voice calm. Even. "Henry's father isn't in the picture. And you already know I'm in trouble. I'm without a job or a place to live." One breath in, another out. "Instead of working on those issues, I'm stuck standing here, being questioned about areas of my life that are none of your concern."

"Right. I know you came here for a job that no longer exists. I don't know why or what happened, but I suppose if you felt like telling me, you would." He waited, as if he thought she'd fill in the blanks. When she didn't, he cleared his throat. "Also, you're not stuck standing here. The door's over there. Feel free to walk through it anytime you please. And I'm sorry for mentioning Henry's father. You're correct. Your personal life isn't my business."

"That's right. It isn't," she said, appreciating his apology but not ready to let go of her temper. "And while I am grateful for all of your assistance, it's time for me and Henry to leave."

"And go where?"

"A motel," she said, hating the idea. Well, she hated all of this. The uncertainty and the unknowns. "I'll just need to see the phone book again, to figure out which one is closest."

"So you can walk there, with all your stuff and Henry?"

"Why not?" Doing so wouldn't be easy, but she'd get the job done. Even if that meant making several trips to and from the restaurant. With Henry. In the still-cold, windy weather.

"That's certainly one possibility, but will you hear me out first?" Dylan asked quietly, in such a tone that she'd be hard-pressed not to agree. "Please?"

And darn it, the *please* finished the job. She gave a short nod.

"It's like this." He spoke fast, as if worried she'd change her mind. "Haley and Henry were hanging out. She mentioned the camp. He asked a few questions about what the boys did while they were there, and he got all pumped over the idea of learning how to raise a tent. My sister offered to teach him, if you gave your permission. That's it, Chelsea."

She took in a lungful of air and gave herself a few seconds to regain her equilibrium. His explanation made sense, and she had no doubt that her son had, indeed, gone over the moon at the idea of learning how to put up a tent. But neither of those facts changed her decision.

"Then I'm sorry, too, for overreacting," she said. "I've been off-kilter since losing my job, and you keep surprising me. But I can't let Haley babysit Henry."

"Why not?" Dylan countered. "Wouldn't it be easier to job hunt and locate living arrangements without Henry tagging along?"

Logically, yes. Emotionally? Not at all. "You and your sister seem very nice, but I don't really know either of you," she said. "And I'm too uncomfortable with having my son somewhere I've never been, with someone I don't really know. That has to make sense to you."

"It does. Completely," he said, without missing a beat. "How about a compromise? Take an hour to go to Haley's with me, see how you feel then. If you become more comfortable, I'll drive you to your motel and wherever else you want to go. If you're not, then I'll do the same, we'll just take Henry with us. Either way, you won't lose any time, since I'll play chauffeur."

Oh, jeez. What to do? She didn't want to give in—not at all—but the thought of disappointing Henry combined with the logic of Dylan's first offer and the wisdom of his second forced her hand. And it would be so much easier to have a ride to the motel.

"I guess I can live with that," she said. "As long as you don't mind playing chauffeur."

"I wouldn't have offered if I minded."

"And that's what I don't understand."

"What is it you don't understand?"

"I… It's just that you keep…" Overwhelmed, she closed her mouth and dropped her gaze to the floor. "I don't understand why you're so kind to someone you don't know."

"It's called lending a helping hand. You're right, we've barely met, but one thing has already become crystal clear," he said, speaking softly. "You question kindness, seemingly at every turn. How is it you've had such bad luck that you can't trust in basic human goodness?"

"How is it that you've had such good luck that you can?" The question flew from her mouth, unbidden, and she wished—oh, how she wished—that she could take it back. She felt visible. Vulnerable. "Never mind. It doesn't matter."

"I think it does. I think you've been taught that trusting in kindness is a mistake."

One long step and he stood in front of her. Close. So close she could lean into him, into his strength, if she so chose. Of course, she didn't. The thought was…entirely unreasonable. Besides which, he was wrong. Kindness had nothing to do with her ability to trust.

She just didn't trust, period.

"Maybe I'm just smart," she said. "Maybe what I've learned is that too many people only care for themselves and what they can get out of any given situation."

He winced slightly, and she wondered if there was a story there, behind that wince.

"I'm sorry for that, for whatever brought you to that conclusion, and it's always smart to be aware," Dylan said. "But I'd like to believe that most people are honestly kind, because most people know that they can't do everything on their own. You gotta know that, too."

Oh, she did. But she was too afraid of all the potential

fallouts to not do everything on her own. And this was not a topic she was prepared to discuss. Ever, really. Particularly now, when her world lay crumbled at her feet and she had zero stability.

Raising her chin a stubborn notch, she said, "If we're going to Haley's, we need to do so now. Otherwise, I'm taking Henry and finding a motel. On my own."

"Sure," he said easily. Another long, intense look passed between them. "You'll have to meet my family first, as they're with Henry at the moment and they'll want to say hi. It's nothing to worry about, and we'll be in and out lightning fast."

No, no, no. Meeting more Fosters was not on her agenda. "Why?"

"Why what?"

"Why do I have to meet them, and why do they care if they meet me?" she asked, speaking slowly and purposefully. "I'm no one to them."

"Ah…because that's how my family is, and I wouldn't say you're no one. They've met your son. They know you stayed the night here and that you're new to Steamboat Springs. Why wouldn't they want to meet you?" Every inch of his body, from his long legs to the straight, even line of his shoulders, tensed. "They're interested and curious. That's all there is to it."

Oh, she was pretty sure there was something more to it, but she couldn't say what. And arguing would only slow her down, whether she won the argument or not. "Fine," she said, choosing the path of least resistance. "So long as it's fast. I mean it, Dylan."

"Fifteen minutes, Chelsea," Dylan said with an easy smile. "And we'll be out of here."

Relieved, she nodded and forced her legs to carry her forward. None of this seemed real. Or sane. Because, despite Dylan's assurances to the contrary, most people did not put themselves out to help strangers. Oh, they might offer their bus seat to an elderly person, or give directions to someone who was lost, or any number of less disruptive acts of kindness.

But everything that had transpired since Dylan had found her in her car last night seemed more than the typical. Kind, yes. Helpful, without a doubt. And she was appreciative.

She just couldn't stop herself from wondering and, okay, worrying if there was more to Dylan Foster and his ready-to-lend-a-hand attitude than met the eye. What was his motivation, because he had to have one, didn't he? Well…unless he was one of those men who couldn't resist fixing other people's problems. Maybe. She didn't like the notion, for many reasons, but the explanation worked well enough to settle her concerns.

Because if that was the type of man he was, he'd move on to the next problem he came across soon enough. Probably within a week, unless she went out of her way to track him down or accidentally bumped into him somewhere, Dylan Foster would've vanished from her life.

And that was fine.

Or…that *should* be fine. Rather, the thought left her feeling distinctly let down.

Thankfully, Dylan's family had been on their best behavior when they met Chelsea. All of them—even Reid— had stuck to the normal, obvious type of questions folks asked when first getting to know someone. This was likely due to Henry's presence, but Dylan didn't care why. He was just pleased they'd gotten in and out as quickly as he'd promised Chelsea they would.

Relieved, too, even if that relief was short-lived. No doubt his brothers were already compiling a list detailing what they wanted to know about Chelsea and why Dylan had taken her under his wing so damn fast. But that was to be dealt with later.

Within fifteen minutes, he'd had Chelsea and Henry in his car and they were following Haley toward her and Gavin's refurbished farmhouse. Their home, and therefore the camp, was located near the top end of a long, windy, uphill road with plenty of acreage and solitude.

For close to a year and a half, the entire Foster crew had worked to get the house and the land ready for the camp's opening this past October. In that time, Dylan had grown close enough to Gavin to consider him a friend, and he guessed soon enough he'd be able to call him a brother, as well. Gavin was a solid, dependable, goal-oriented man who was, in many ways, a complete opposite from Haley and her fly-by-the-seat-of-her-pants approach to life.

Strange as it might sound, they were a good match.

Now the two men were sitting on the farmhouse's wide enclosed back porch, enjoying mugs of strong black coffee, watching as Haley expertly demonstrated how to raise a tent to an avid audience of three: Henry, Chelsea and the camp's mascot, a pooch of unknown origins named Roxie. Chelsea and Henry were paying close attention as Haley spoke, but the dog seemed more interested in running in excited circles around the group. Every now and then, she'd stop and playfully butt her head against Henry's legs.

"Everything going well with you guys?" Dylan asked Gavin, more to fill the silence than anything else. If there was trouble in paradise, he'd already know about it.

"Yeah, it is. Life is good."

And that was another aspect of Gavin's personality that Dylan enjoyed: he didn't mince words or overly explain. "I'm glad. It's nice to see Haley as happy as she is. So…ah, how quickly did you know she was someone to pay attention to?"

Damn. Where had that question come from?

"I don't know that I had much choice but to pay attention." Shifting in his seat, Gavin switched his focus to Dylan. "You know how your sister is when she sets her sights on something. She isn't an easy person to ignore. She was rather focused on being seen."

"That's my sister. My parents should have named her Haley Tenacious Foster."

"Yup. Though I'd say she comes by the trait naturally. Didn't take me long to figure that one out." Gavin tapped his coffee mug with his thumb. "Tenacious, determined, stubborn as the day is long. I'd say that describes the entire Foster family to a T."

"The rest of them, maybe. Me? I tend to be on the more laid-back side."

Gavin laughed. A rough, tough, gravelly type of a sound that completely matched his six-foot-five height and linebacker build. "Laid-back? Nah. Hate to tell you this, my friend, but that word isn't even in the dictionary as far as you're concerned."

Surprised and somewhat ill at ease, Dylan sat up straighter. "What are you talking about? I'm about as laid-back as you can get. I think you're confusing me with my brothers."

"You can think what you want, and you put on a pretty good show." Gavin laughed again, louder this time, as if he'd just heard the greatest joke ever told. "But as good as you are at pretending, it's still nothing but a show."

"In what way?"

The other man blinked. "Seriously? You're sure you want me to go into this?"

"I have no idea what you mean. So yeah, seriously."

"Okay." Gavin glanced toward the women and Henry and, seeing they were only about halfway through the raising-a-tent lesson, nodded. "Back when I was a kid and stuck in the foster-care system, the only way to feel like life hadn't handed you a full basket of rotten, stinking eggs was to put on an I-don't-care attitude. Life is great. I'm great. Don't want a damn thing I don't already have." Shrugging, Gavin finished off his coffee and set the mug on the porch's wood-planked floor. "You remind me of those days. Of myself and the other boys."

Dylan didn't respond right off. Couldn't for a few different reasons. One, he had never heard so many words come from Gavin's mouth so quickly. Two, while the other man's interpretation didn't offend him, he found it troubling. Wrong, though.

"I know you had it tough growing up." Swallowing down the rest of his coffee, Dylan chose his next words carefully. "And I can't imagine what it took to get through those years, but my life in no way compares to what you had to deal with."

"True enough." Gavin rubbed his hand over his short, trimmed beard. "This is getting deep, and hell, this isn't my business. But…"

"But?"

"Don't get me wrong. I don't think you're this unhappy guy or anything. You're aware of what's good in your life. I just think…" Pausing, Gavin gave his head a slight shake. "You know, when I met Haley, I had all these self-constructed barriers in place. Last thing I wanted was to let any of them drop or admit I wanted more. Safer that way, even though I knew the whole damn time I was only kidding myself. I did want more, but going there meant risking the safe, sane life I'd finally put together. And it could be that you're not ready to hear this, but I sort of think that's where you're at. Where you've been for a while."

Dylan let Gavin's words settle for a minute, maybe

two, before he shook his head in rejection of the whole damn concept. "You're thinking too much," he said. "I'm an open book. What you see is what you get, and I'm not pretending I'm happy. I actually am happy."

"Yeah, well, took me a while to face the truth. Took me longer to do something about it." Then, saving both men from the protracted, uncomfortable moment that was sure to follow such a speech, he flashed an easy grin and said, "I could use more coffee right about now. You?"

"Sure. Another jolt of caffeine would be great." He'd use the opportunity to check in with Reid about the possible job opening at the pediatrician's office. He hoped that one came through, because Cole had already sent him a text stating that Dee's Deli was no longer in need of another employee. "After that, though, we'll have to head out. Chelsea needs to find a job quick-like."

If the doctor's office fell through and none of his family had sniffed out any new leads, Dylan might have to do something crazy and…well, he didn't know what he'd do, exactly.

"About that," Gavin said, leading them inside and straight into the large open kitchen. "Haley called on the way here to share what's going on, and we had an idea that might work for Chelsea and would solve a temporary problem for us. It's probably not a permanent fix, but if she agrees and it all pans out, it would give her some breathing room."

"Oh, yeah?" Interest piqued, Dylan handed Gavin his empty coffee cup and leaned against one of the kitchen counters. "Why didn't Haley mention this suggestion earlier?"

"A couple of reasons. The main one is she wanted to talk with me, get my take, which shows you how far she's come. In the past, she would've listened to her heart without considering anything else, jumped right in and let the chips fall wherever they landed."

"Yup, that sounds like Haley."

Gavin poured them each a fresh cup of coffee. After handing Dylan his mug, he said, "And I suppose the fact that I didn't instantly consider a million ways the idea could go wrong shows how far I've come. Regardless, I think her plan has enough merit to consider."

"I could use a plan with merit," Dylan said. Maybe luck was with him and Chelsea's problems would be solved today, after all. If so, she'd be set and he'd be able to… what? Forget he ever met her? Yeah. That. "And I'm definitely intrigued. Tell me what you have in mind."

"Can't. Not yet." Gavin nodded toward the window. "Some of what led to this idea was meant to be a surprise, and it's Haley's call how much we give away. Best if we wait for her so I'm not stuck sleeping on the couch. I just wanted to give you a heads-up."

Not much of a heads-up, but Dylan didn't object. His thoughts returned to his earlier conversation with Gavin and his…theories, he guessed he'd call them. Wrong. Dead wrong, all of them. Dylan not only enjoyed his uncomplicated life, he friggin' treasured it. He wasn't faking a damn thing. He didn't want *anything* he didn't have.

Without so much as a millisecond's pause after that thought, he cocked his head toward the window, stared out and his eyes instantly found Chelsea. She was smiling at Henry, who had gotten into a tug-of-war with the dog over a stick. Again, the sight of her and the boy warmed his heart, softened his defenses, and out of nowhere, all sorts of possibilities rammed into his brain.

Perhaps—and he'd have to give this a helluva lot more thought—he did want more, at that. But even if he came to that conclusion, that didn't necessarily equate to Chelsea being the solution or that going after more was worth the inherent risk.

It likely wasn't. Almost certainly was not. But what if…just what if it was?

Chapter Six

"I want to go camping now!" Henry exclaimed, his little body vibrating with excitement. "We know how to build a tent and we can have a campfire and toast marshmallows and sleep in bags on the ground and look up at the stars and make wishes. Can we do that, Mommy? Please?"

"Um...sure. Someday, we can," Chelsea said. While the past thirty minutes had been pleasant enough, her thoughts weren't centered on camping with her son. The pressure to locate some solid footing kept her from fully enjoying herself. "Not today, of course. It's far too cold out here for camping. Maybe this summer, though."

Henry frowned and stubbed his sneaker-covered toe into the snow. "I know what *maybe* and *someday* means. We prolly won't go camping this summer or ever."

"Hey, I didn't say that, sweetie." Chelsea pulled her son close for a hug. "How about this? I *promise* we'll go camping sometime this summer."

"Really?" he asked, his face buried against her coat. "You promise?"

"I'll even cross my heart." He looked up to meet her gaze with his. She smiled and his blue eyes regained their brightness, and his expression of pure joy meant everything in the world to her.

"Don't forget the marshmallows!"

"Camping wouldn't be camping without marshmallows," Haley said. She patted the dog, Roxie, on the head and nodded toward the house. "Let's go inside and warm up. There's something me and Gavin would like to talk over with you, Chelsea."

"Oh, is this about watching Henry? Because I'm fine with the idea now." Obviously, Haley was good with kids, just as Dylan had said, and Henry hadn't had such a carefree experience in too long a while. She wouldn't insist he come with her for a no-fun day when he could stay here and be a kid. "If you're still willing to watch him, that is."

"Of course I'm willing! But there's something else I'd like to discuss." Haley twisted a long strand of hair around one gloved finger. "Come inside, and I'll get a snack for Henry and we can sit in front of the fire. And I'll explain what I'm thinking."

Chelsea pushed up her coat sleeve to glance at her watch. "I'm sorry. I really can't."

"Aw, come on. You can spare a few extra minutes for the gracious, lovely young woman who's babysitting Henry, can't you?"

If it weren't for the lighthearted manner in which Haley had spoken, Chelsea would've taken offense. Teasing or not, though, Haley had put her straight in front of a roadblock. She couldn't refuse Haley any easier than she'd managed to refuse Dylan. "Of course I can," she said after a moment's pause. "Sitting in front of the fire sounds nice."

"Smart, giving in so fast," Haley said, her lips quirking into a grin. "You wouldn't know this yet, but I tend to get my way when something is important."

Curious and confused—another state of affairs that seemed to occur on a regular basis with the Fosters—she reached for Henry's mitten-covered hand and followed Haley toward the house, all the while trying to keep her anxiety at bay. Difficult to do, though.

Chelsea could almost feel the clock's hands ticking away, and as each second passed, her hope for accomplishing any of what she had to do that day diminished. She should have put her foot down with Dylan to begin with, politely, and gone on her way as planned.

It wasn't too late to change course. The second she could do so, she'd ask Dylan to drop her off at the Mountain Peaks Motel, which happened to be a somewhat easy walk to a decent number of Steamboat Springs businesses. She'd then pound the pavement for work and, if they were open, stop in at the couple of day-care establishments she'd found in the phone book.

Her hope was to establish a payment arrangement until she was more flush. A doubtful hope, most likely, but she had to try. She just kept telling herself that, somehow, everything she needed would come together by the time she met up with Henry at Foster's early that evening.

Now inside, Haley pointed in the direction of the living room, saying, "Why don't you take off your coat and sit down, Chelsea? I'll get Henry settled with a snack and be right in."

Pursing her lips, Chelsea let out a breath. "I'm really in a hurry, Haley, so—"

"I know you think you are, but I'm guessing that will change real fast." With that, Haley tugged on Henry's hand and led him away, leaving Chelsea to do as she was instructed.

Shrugging off her coat, she entered the living room and…stopped. Breathed again, and some of her tension drained away. What a room.

A large stone fireplace instantly stole her attention. It sat against the longest wall, directly in the center, with a welcoming fire already burning. Various framed photos were arranged on the cedar mantel, compelling Chelsea to walk closer for a better view.

All of them were of the Fosters, in various groupings and poses. Some outside, some in. The siblings, including Dylan, standing at the base of a mountain with skis leveraged on their shoulders and happy smiles on their faces. There was one of—Reid? Yes, that was Reid. She'd only spent a few minutes with him earlier, but she recognized the oldest brother's serious, focused gaze—and a woman with vibrant red hair on what had to be their wedding day.

Next, she saw Cole—who greatly resembled Reid with the same dark eyes and hair—and a beautiful blonde woman, her head pressed against his shoulder and his arm wrapped tightly around her waist. Both couples appeared blissful. Moving on, Chelsea smiled at the sight of two tiny babies—likely only a month or so old when the photo was taken—curled beside each other, their tiny fingers entwined. Twins? Had to be. And, based on the strawberry blond fuzz covering the infants' heads, she guessed they belonged to Reid and his wife.

Directly next to the picture of the babies was one of the senior Fosters, Paul and Margaret. They were both smiling, naturally, but there was an air of confidence and contentedness surrounding them that made it seem as if they'd always been together. Belonged together. Finally, Chelsea settled her gaze on a photograph of Gavin and Haley. This one held the centermost position on the mantel, and they were shown sitting outside amid a cluster of trees—probably somewhere on their property—with that silly dog in between them.

A sigh born of deep longing escaped from Chelsea's lungs. What she'd wanted, had yearned for, her entire life existed right here in front of her. *Family*. In the Fosters. And due to a set of unforeseen circumstances, here she stood, surrounded by them. Surrounded by family.

Just not *her* family.

At best, she could call Dylan and Haley—maybe Margaret, as well—friendly acquaintances. She didn't think her speedy introductions to Reid, Cole, Paul and now Gavin were enough to move them past the stranger phase, and heck, she didn't even know the names of the women or the babies in the photos. Just the same, she suddenly felt as if she knew them all.

Or, perhaps, as if she were *meant* to know all of them, and that was why she'd lost her job, why her car had broken down and why she was even standing in this room now.

Right. As if fate would go to such extreme lengths to ensure she'd meet Dylan and his family. Pushing the ridiculous thought out of her head, Chelsea retreated to the sofa, where she laid her coat over one of the arms and sat down.

She looked at her watch and her anxiety returned, twisting and turning inside of her, causing a wash of nausea. What was she doing here? She'd give Haley another five minutes, max, before she'd go in search of her, apologize and ask Dylan to take her to the motel.

Almost as if he'd read her mind, Dylan chose that second to enter the living room. Her mouth went dry and her heart picked up an extra beat. She ignored both annoying reactions and said, "Do you know what Haley and Gavin want to talk to me about?"

"Not really." He sat down in one of the two overstuffed

chairs across from the sofa and stretched his legs in front of him. "Gavin would only say so much without Haley's input. It was—" a somewhat sheepish expression appeared "—rather frustrating, actually. I'm sorry about this. You must be champing at the bit to get moving."

"I am." No reason to say more. He already knew her position.

A quick, chirpy series of beeps sounded off, causing Dylan to reach into the pocket of his jeans. He retrieved his cell, slid his finger across the smartphone's screen and, apparently disliking whatever it was he read, frowned.

"Everything okay?" Chelsea asked.

"Hmm? Oh, yeah. I'm good." He tapped his finger on the back of the cell phone's case. "If I suggest something, will you promise to listen before jumping to crazy conclusions?"

Oh, jeez. Now what? "I'll listen, sure. I'll even promise that whatever conclusion I reach won't seem crazy to me. But I can't promise that you won't see it that way."

Nodding, he tucked his phone into his jeans. "Finding a job might take more time than one afternoon, and I have the sense you're out here on your own, with no one to call on for help." He paused, exhaled a breath. "Is that a correct assumption?"

"I do fine on my own," she said, declining to share any specifics. Why did it matter to him, anyway? "But I'll find a job. Today or tomorrow or the next day."

Please, please let it be today.

"I hope you do. Really. But in case you don't, I'd like to offer you a loan—" he held up a hand, as if anticipating her response "—and I'd like you to consider accepting it."

"Really? Dylan, I don't think—"

"I'm not done, and you said you'd listen." At her nod, he continued with "I keep thinking about Haley and how if she was stuck in a strange city I'd want someone to lend a hand." His expression stilled, grew serious. "That's all this is, Chelsea. I'll feel better as a person knowing that you and Henry have enough stability to get back on your feet."

She waited for, and expected, her defensive attitude to rear its ugly head. But it didn't. Maybe comparing her situation to his sister helped, or maybe she was just too mentally worn down to argue. Oh, she wasn't about to accept. Not now, hopefully not at all. But if everything went even more downhill and she had no other option, well… she'd consider it then.

"I might eventually have to take you up on that," she said, managing to keep her voice even and clear. "For now, though, I'll stick with my plan. This is my problem, not yours."

"Didn't say it was my problem, but—" Dylan leaned forward, minimizing the space between them, and said, "—I won't argue, so long as you keep the offer in mind."

"I will." Silence loomed between them, so she added, "I promise."

"Good." His lips stretched into a smile. "It did not escape my attention, by the way, that you didn't instantly jump to crazy conclusions. Thanks for that."

"Kind of a weird thing to thank someone for, especially since you just offered me a loan, but you're welcome." Silence returned, but he didn't retreat to his prior kicked-back position. His focus remained wholly centered on her, his gaze steady and sure. It was hard, but she resisted the strong compulsion to look away. "Um…is there something else on your mind?"

"Tons," he said. "Most of which have to do with you. Like…where was your home before you decided to move here? Did you purposely look for a job in Steamboat Springs, or was the city the result of the job? Why leave home for a place where you don't know a single soul?

And the question really weighing on my mind the most, why are you alone?"

There had been a chance, if he hadn't asked the last, she might have answered one or two of the former. Chelsea didn't care if Dylan knew she was born and raised in Pueblo. Didn't bother her all that much to admit she'd moved here due to the job and not the other way around. But asking why she was alone, with such surety that she was, indeed, alone?

She clasped her hands together and tried to turn her head, to escape from the penetrating, inquisitive scrutiny of his stare. But she couldn't. Dylan's final question hung in the air, solid and inescapable, leaving her caught as securely as a fly in a sticky spider's web.

Even if her life depended on her giving a response, she did not know how to connect the words together in such a way that he—that *anyone*—could understand. And the concept of even trying was enough to tie her tongue into knots. What really did it, though, was the realization that she had become so obviously, unquestionably alone that this man had seen it for himself.

Swallowing past the thick layer coating her throat, she said, "Henry does that, too. He'll ask ten questions without waiting for an answer from the first. Of course, Henry is four."

Dylan's gaze still didn't waver, but his jaw tensed, and she couldn't help but notice the muscle there begin to twitch. "You really don't like giving away personal details, do you?"

She opened her mouth—to say what, she didn't know—and closed it again. He didn't say anything else, either. But they stayed that way, looking at each other in weighted silence, for what seemed like hours upon hours but was likely only a matter of seconds, before Haley and Gavin came into the room. And wow, was Chelsea grateful.

"Okay, I have Henry all set with some cookies and milk and, for when he's done, a coloring book and crayons," Haley was saying. "He should be content for long enough to have this conversation. After that, we'll see where we're at."

"Thank you," Chelsea murmured, her encounter with Dylan leaving her dazed. "I'm, um, flabbergasted he didn't wheedle you into giving him soda with the cookies."

"Oh, he tried." Gavin sat in the other chair and motioned to Haley, who plopped onto his lap as if it were the most natural thing in the world. "But I gave him his choices as cookies and milk, or he could have the soda, but then he'd get carrot sticks to balance the sugar."

"Not a shocker he went with the cookies and milk," she said. "Though, if you'd given him ranch dressing for the carrot sticks, he probably would've thought that was a fair deal."

Again, a sense of familiarity stole in, as if sitting here with these people had happened many times in the past. As if it would again in the future. Rather than increasing her comfort, however, the realization felt almost threatening. Because it wasn't true.

"I hope this doesn't come off as rude," she said, "but what is it you want to talk about?"

"Before we can fully explain, I need to drag a promise from my brother," Haley said. "Well, you, too, but it's Dylan I'm most concerned with, since it involves keeping a secret."

"Since when am I a blabbermouth?" Dylan asked, sounding somewhat insulted. "I've kept plenty of secrets for you in the past, Haley. More than our brothers, I'm sure."

"You're not a blabbermouth," Haley confirmed. "But this is really important, and there can't be any gray areas. None. So that means you can't tell anyone what you're about to hear, even if you disagree with our reasons. And I need you to promise."

"Depends," Dylan said, his voice holding notes of concern. "Is this a good thing?"

"Now, it shouldn't matter one way or the other," Gavin said. "Because you should know we wouldn't ask you to stay hush on something that could hurt anyone. But for the record, we think it's rather good. And we hope you'll feel the same."

"Well, that's an easy enough promise to make, then," Dylan said. "So, yeah, I promise."

"Thank you!" Haley grinned. "Chelsea?"

"Um. Sure, I promise not to tell anyone." Really, though, who *would* she tell?

"That's what we needed to hear, so I think we're all set." Haley reached for Gavin's hand and inhaled a deep breath. "Gavin and I have decided to throw a surprise wedding. Next month. Here, outside if the weather cooperates, and it will be small. We'll invite everyone for a barbecue and then when they're here, we'll announce that we're getting married instead."

Dylan's jaw dropped open. "A surprise wedding? Oh… wait a minute. This is what you were all secretive about last night, isn't it? That thing you said I wouldn't find exciting? Because my sister getting married? Kind of exciting."

"Yes. And sorry about that, but you have this annoying way of getting into people's heads." Haley grinned at her brother. "Now that you know, what do you think?"

"I'm happy for you two, without a doubt."

"But?" Haley said. "I know you have a *but* hidden there somewhere."

"*However*, I think the surprise factor could potentially hurt our parents' feelings," Dylan said. "You're their only daughter, Haley. Mom will want to shop for the dress with you, help with whatever plans need to be made. Dad will want to help foot the cost, if not the whole shebang. Why not have a wedding everyone can be a part of from the get-go?"

"I'm wearing Mom's wedding dress, supposing I can find it easy enough, so there won't be any dress shopping," Haley said quickly. "And we don't want Dad to pay for anything."

"There won't be much to pay for," Gavin said, taking over the conversation. "The guest list is small, minimizing the cost of food and drink. Our venue is here, so that's free, and we just don't want a lot of fuss. We want a simple, fun celebration."

"Okay, but why can't you have all of that and let the family in on the news? Everyone will be fine with whatever you two want," Dylan said. "You know that's true."

"It is true, but weddings have a habit of getting out of control, of becoming a lot more about the presentation and the...the frills, I guess. Our wedding is going to be about what *we're* grateful for, and we want to share that with our family and friends," Haley said, her tone emphatic. "Our decision is set. But it would mean the world to have your support."

"You have that, in spades," Dylan said instantly. "And I'll help however I can."

Haley leaped off of Gavin's lap and held her arms out to her brother. He stood and crushed her into a hug. When they separated, she said, "Thank you, big brother."

Chelsea watched and listened with interest, but couldn't understand what any of this had to do with her or why Haley and Gavin had decided to bring her into the discussion. Refraining from glancing at her watch again, she said, "Congratulations! I'm also happy for you two. And I hope the wedding is beautiful. Now, though, I need to—"

"Hold on. We're not done," Gavin said. "Now we can get to the part that involves you."

Returning to Gavin's lap, Haley grinned at Chelsea. "Dylan mentioned that you're in need of a job, and we'd like to offer you one. Temporary to start. And because we'd need you to be here while we're on our honeymoon, room and board. We can't pay a lot, but—"

"Wait a minute…what?" This came from Dylan, but his question and confused tone expressed Chelsea's thoughts and feelings perfectly.

A job offer, room and board, *and* a small salary? It seemed too good to be true.

"It's simple," Gavin said. "There's a lot of work and planning to do for the camp before the first group of boys arrives in June. Unless we have someone here who can deal with the administrative necessities as they come up, we won't be able to have a honeymoon."

"But this isn't only about the wedding," Haley said. "Beginning in October, the number of campers will increase. This means stricter guidelines, which means more paperwork, more fund-raising needs, more…everything. I need an extra set of hands, period. We just want to be sure we have the right fit. So, what we're offering is a temporary, part-time position to begin, but with the possibility of becoming full-time and permanent. Assuming all goes well."

At those words, Chelsea sat up a little straighter. Oh, Lord, this could be her saving grace.

"Got it," Dylan said, his voice sharp. "I understand the necessities, but I don't know if offering the position to Chelsea so fast is well thought out. She…that is, she could be a…I don't know, a nefarious diamond-and-gold-nugget thief, on the lam. Or an ax murderer!" He cringed. "Perhaps not either of those, but I think you're jumping the gun."

"Diamond-and-gold-nugget thief?" Haley grinned in pure delight. "Are you on the lam, Chelsea? Or do you go around murdering innocent folks with big, bad axes?"

"Nope. I only murder guilty folks, and my ax is rather dainty and small." She gave Dylan a dirty look. What was with him? One second he was trying to throw money at her, and the next he was throwing her under the bus. "I'm neither a thief nor an ax-wielding serial killer, and if I was on the lam, I'd go somewhere warm. With a beach."

Dylan swiped his hand over his forehead. "That was rude. My sister offered you her home and she tends to— in the past, I mean—wear her heart on her sleeve. I over-reacted."

"Out of protection and concern." This was a response that Chelsea understood. Finally. "Maybe what you meant to say is that my résumé and references should be consid-ered before an employment offer is made? That would be a logical sequence of events, would it not?"

"Ah, yeah. That would be logical."

"But see, this is why you came into our lives at the per-fect moment," Haley said to Chelsea. "The wedding isn't until mid-May, which is weeks and weeks away. By the time we leave for our honeymoon, you'll be up to speed on the necessities, and as a bonus, you won't require child care. We think it's an ideal solution all the way around."

The theme song from *The Twilight Zone* played in Chel-sea's head. Was this fate or blind, dumb luck, or some-thing else entirely? She didn't know. This could be—no, it was—exactly what she and Henry needed. Their chance at a brand-new fresh start.

"I would love to say yes." Chelsea spoke quickly, be-fore Dylan could declare her a bank robber, as well. She understood his prior response, but she *needed* this to hap-pen. "*If* you feel the same after reviewing my résumé and references. If not, we'll just agree this isn't the right fit."

"Sounds like a deal to me," Gavin said. "Dylan?"

"Not my call, but that…ah…seems reasonable."

"Well, what are we waiting for? Let's see your résumé," Haley said as she stood. "Because the sooner we get this settled, the sooner I can show you to your bedrooms!"

This was really happening. A job and a home—Chelsea looked over to the fireplace's mantel, to the framed photographs, and a sense of belonging, of family, filled her heart. Nope, not her family, but maybe this job, here with Gavin and Haley, would help her in far greater measures than any other job ever would. Maybe fate had a hand in this, after all.

"Chelsea?" Dylan's voice pulled her back to the present, to him. "What bag is your résumé in? I'll go out to the car and grab it for you."

"Oh. Um." She shook her head to clear her thoughts and focused on Dylan. He looked better now. Not nearly as stressed. Maybe he'd already gotten over his qualms? She hoped so. "It's in the outside pocket of the purple suitcase. The upright. In a file folder. But I can get it."

"Nah, stay here and chat with Gavin and Haley. Find out more about the job."

She nodded and watched as he left the room. If she was here due to fate, then Dylan stood in the center of it all. Because none of this would have happened without him. He'd found her in her car. He'd offered her and Henry a safe haven for the night. He'd convinced her to come here today. He'd tried to lend her money, not once but twice. And he… Oh. Wow.

Last night, he'd offered to talk to his family about scrounging up some temporary work she could do for them. He'd even brought up the possibility of finding somewhere better than a cheap motel for Henry and her to sleep. She'd said no, firmly and decisively, yet suddenly, this perfect job offer from *his sister* presented itself, which miraculously included room and board.

Chelsea's heart dropped. She should've clued in to this immediately.

Dylan and his Good Samaritan nature had orchestrated this entire thing. This had to be his doing…except, well, he'd truly seemed uncomfortable when Haley had mentioned the opportunity, and his reaction had definitely fallen on the bizarre side. Was that a show, put on for her benefit? Chelsea didn't know, couldn't know, for sure, but…darn it, that seemed more likely than fate bringing her here, to him and to this house, to this job.

Fate had never been so kind to her before, so why in the hell would it start now?

She didn't need charity. Well, maybe in this exact moment she did, but she didn't want it and she didn't see how she could accept. Unless…she just went along with it, for now. She'd do the best job she could, more than enough to prove her worth—because she really believed Gavin and Haley were planning on hiring *someone*—and when the gig ended, she'd move on.

By then, she'd be in a stronger position financially, would likely have located a place for her and Henry to call home, and hopefully, permanent employment, as well.

Maybe Foster kindness had brought her this opportunity, but she'd make damn sure that when all was said and done, she'd earned her pay and her keep. It wouldn't feel like charity then, to her or to Gavin and Haley. No one else mattered in the equation.

As far as Dylan Foster went, however, she now knew enough to keep him at a long arm's distance. His presence alone made her want to believe in something more than she'd ever had, and his arguments about trusting in the kindness of others made her want to believe in *him*.

Dangerous ground to step onto with anyone. Scary, too.

But with a man who only saw her as a problem requiring a solution? Impossible.

Settled with both of her decisions, she nodded at Gavin and Haley. "While we're waiting, why don't you tell me more about the camp? And what you're looking for in the way of help? If this ends up working out, I promise you won't regret giving me this chance."

This was *not* what he'd wanted. Well. Okay, it was what he'd wanted as far as some of the particulars went. Dylan should feel pleased with the turn of events. Chelsea was set for the time being. She had the breathing room required to get her to a better place, even if she moved on after Gavin and Haley returned from their honeymoon.

But he hadn't wanted Chelsea to be ensconced in his sister's home. Not because he thought she was a thief, as he'd stupidly blurted. The truth was, when his sister had offered the job, every last thing he didn't know about Chelsea came into sharp, blaring focus.

Such as, what was the job she'd lost, and why had she lost it? Where had Chelsea and Henry called home before leaving everything behind to come here? Why had she made that choice? And, yeah, where was Henry's father? Or her family? Or…anyone?

Now it infuriated him even more that he'd asked her, directly, several of those very same questions and she'd refused to answer. She hadn't even bothered giving him pat replies.

Dylan popped open the trunk of his car, questions slamming into his brain one after another. Seeing the purple suitcase, he unzipped the side pocket and retrieved the file folder. He didn't think if he should or he shouldn't, just opened the file folder to read her résumé.

Pueblo, Colorado. That was her home. And her most recent position had been as a waitress at a diner, where she'd worked for close to a year. Before that, she'd had a short stint—less than six months—with a temporary employment agency and before that as a customer service operator at an insurance company. That one she'd had for slightly over two years, but the job had been eliminated due to the company going the way of technology and choosing to use an automated telephone service rather than actual human beings.

And before that, it appeared as if she'd worked part-time while going to school part-time. He had to guess, based on the dates shown and Henry's age, that her pregnancy with him had halted her ability to continue college. Dylan felt bad. Really bad, actually, because on this résumé, he saw a woman who had struggled to find her way.

So, okay. Chances were high that she'd come to Steamboat Springs for exactly the reason he'd heard—a brand-new fresh start—but that didn't answer all of his other questions. And the knowledge gained from reading her résumé didn't lessen his reborn uneasiness.

Now that Chelsea would be so damn close to his family, to him, he couldn't ignore his disquiet. He couldn't step away and let distance work its magic, nor could he entertain the idea of seeing where his interest in her might lead. Not while she lived with his sister, at any rate. Not without knowing what she was made of. Because, if for some reason, she had an agenda unknown to him or, hell, secrets that could be damaging to those near her, the fall-out could affect his family. And that was something he could not, would not, allow.

He cursed loudly and slammed the trunk shut. Idiotic to allow a woman to crawl into his life and past his defenses once again. At least with Elise, he'd known her history. He'd known her family. He understood what demons had haunted her. None of that excused her eventual behavior or his inability to clue in and see what was really happening, but he couldn't say he'd gone in completely blind, either. His heart had led, not his brain.

Dylan strode toward the house with a new goal in mind. One way or another, he'd get his questions answered, and he'd do so without being swayed by Chelsea's various charms. Not her depths-of-the-ocean blue eyes that seemed to hold, all at once, sadness and fear and hope. Not the sultry yet somehow sweet quality to her voice. Not the adorable way she'd lift her chin in mule-headed stubbornness. And no, not even her too-smart-for-his-age, cuter-than-cute kid.

This time he'd lead with his brain, and his heart could just shut the hell up.

Chapter Seven

"Ready for breakfast?" Chelsea asked Henry the next morning. They were in his new bedroom, complete with *two* bunk beds, which had thrilled Henry. He'd almost been beside himself with the realization that he had *four* beds to choose from and that he could select a different bed each and every night if he so chose.

Even better to his four-year-old mind was the dresser drawer full of flashlights. Gavin had explained that, as a child, he'd hated the first few nights in a new foster home. He hadn't known his surroundings, so that made it difficult if he had to find the bathroom in the dark. Therefore, with that memory firmly in place, he'd stocked flashlights in each of the two bedrooms the campers would stay in while they bunked at the house.

It was, Chelsea thought, a sad tale with a sweet ending.

"Can't I just stay in here and play?" Henry asked, looking up from the various toy trucks and cars he'd brought to the center of the room. In addition to the flashlights and bunk beds, the room housed two large toy boxes and a tall bookshelf, both of which looked to be handmade and both filled to capacity. "I'm not hungry yet and this is more fun than breakfast!"

There were plenty of valid reasons to insist Henry follow her downstairs, but he'd been pulled and tugged in so many directions lately, she just didn't have the heart. Let him play. Breakfast could wait. "Sure," she said. "Keep having fun, sweetie, and I'll come get you in an hour. Or if you decide you're ready to eat before then, come downstairs and find me."

"Okay, Mommy. Thanks!" He returned his attention to the pileup and, selecting a toy police car, rolled it forward and said in a booming voice, "You're under arrest! No one move!"

She grinned and left the room. As she walked toward the stairs, she heard Henry mimicking the sound of a police siren as, she guessed, the cop car gave chase. It was wonderful, experiencing her son's childhood elation and being relaxed enough to enjoy the moment.

The job offer had become definite once Haley and Gavin had looked over her résumé. Oh, she was sure that her employment history wasn't a perfect match to what they required, but they must have decided she was, at the very least, trainable. And her reference letters were good enough to satisfy both of them, though she assumed either Gavin or Haley would follow up with phone calls or emails within the next few days. She wasn't concerned, though.

She'd earned the positive remarks in those reference letters by working hard, keeping her head down and being as reliable as possible with a small child.

So long as nothing wacky occurred, she was set.

Downstairs now, Chelsea found Haley in the kitchen. The woman was sitting at the long rectangular table sipping orange juice. In front of her was a container of yogurt, a half-eaten bowl of cereal and a spread-open notebook with a mile-long handwritten list she seemed to be reading. Her hair—the same reddish-brown shade as Dylan's—was bunched in a loose knot on top of her head, with long, wavy strands framing her face. Gavin was nowhere to be seen.

"Good morning," Chelsea said as she approached the table. She spied the full pot of coffee on the counter and wondered if she was free to serve herself. No. Better wait until the rules were established. Instead, she took a chair across from Haley. "Henry is too enamored with the array of toys in his room to be bothered with breakfast just yet. But don't worry. He'll let me know when he's hungry, and I'm ready to start work whenever you are."

"Wow, that's quite the speech," Haley said with a welcoming smile. "And good morning to you." She put down her orange juice and with the same hand gestured toward the fridge. "This is your home now, so help yourself to whatever you'd like. And I'm glad Henry's having such a good time, but no worries. You're not on the clock today."

"Ah…what do you mean I'm not on the clock?" Suddenly, Chelsea wasn't as sure about being set as she had been a few seconds ago. "It's Monday. I assumed you'd want to get started."

"And that would make sense, wouldn't it?" Haley swirled her spoon in the yogurt. "We're so behind schedule that Gavin and I thought it best to hold off on training until we're more caught up. Our goal is to be ready for you by next week. We thought, to make it easier with Henry, we'd try four to five hours a day, Monday through Friday. So twenty to twenty-five hours each week. Does that sound good for you?"

"Yeah. That's great." Ready for her? "Is there a problem I should be concerned with?"

"Oh, no! It's nothing like that. We just finished the winter season, here at the camp and at my family's businesses, so there's a ton to do before we can move on to preparing for summer. Paperwork, mostly. Inventory. Some marketing I have to deal with, updating the various websites and such." Haley tapped her finger on the notebook. "A few repairs on our property—that's where Gavin's at now, and…well, there's just a lot."

"I can help. I'm here now, why not put me to use?"

"Again, that would seem to make sense, wouldn't it?" Haley sighed. "The truth is, it will be quicker for us to dredge through what needs to be done and then focus our attention on setting up for summer. That's where you'll come in. Easier to train you from point A rather than from somewhere toward the end, which is where we're at now. Please, please don't take any of this the wrong way. We really are thrilled you're here! We're just a little unprepared."

"No, no. I get it." And she did. But she couldn't sit around for a full week and pretend she was on vacation. That *would* make her feel as if she and Henry were charity cases, which was not the way she wanted this endeavor to begin. "How about this? Until you're ready, I can help with some of the household chores. Cooking, cleaning, laundry? Does that sound fair?"

"Oh, no, you don't. I mean, if you feel like cooking one night, I won't argue, but we didn't hire you to be our maid. Clean up after yourself and Henry, and we'll be good. Besides," Haley said with a mischievous grin, "Dylan has decided to show you and Henry around Steamboat Springs. He should be here any minute now, actually."

Butterflies. Again. At the merest *mention* of Dylan.

"No, that isn't necessary! I can stay busy and Henry loves his room and there's absolutely no reason for Dylan to go out of his way or…" *Talk slower*, Chelsea ordered herself. She inhaled a calming breath. "That is, I don't want to be a bother."

"Why, you're blushing!" The green in Haley's eyes darkened with curiosity. "That's cute…and interesting. My brother, however, doesn't seem to think you're a bother. This was his idea, and he was quite determined when he called this morning. Insistent, even." Haley's eyes narrowed in speculation. "And now that I think about it, that's interesting, too."

"I just don't understand why he'd… Doesn't he have as much to do as you and Gavin? At the restaurant, I mean, with end-of-the-season responsibilities and such?"

"Oh, he does. Which is another interesting point, isn't it? Is it possible that he's…?" She paused, shook her head. Gnawed on her lip for a few seconds. Then, as if she'd reached some decision unknown to Chelsea, Haley bestowed her with a huge grin. "Don't worry about Dylan. I'm sure he's worked out his schedule to everyone's satisfaction. And once I told him you were free until next Monday, he started making plans for the whole week. You should be plenty busy."

The week? As in seven days? Great. Just freaking great.

And she, apparently, had no say in the matter. How was she to keep Dylan a long arm's distance away, and her unwanted reactions toward him at a minimum, if he had declared himself to be her tour guide for an entire week? No. There had to be a way out.

Trying again, she said, "That's nice. Really nice. But I'd rather stay here and help however I can. Maybe you'll come up with something I can do. Something you're not even thinking of right now. The wedding plans! I can help with those." Haley watched her with that same steady gaze she'd already experienced time and again with Dylan. "Even if my official job doesn't start until next week, you're still giving me and my son room and board. Right?"

"Which you'll more than earn," Haley said matter-of-factly. "Beginning *next* Monday. And while I might ask for your opinion here and there as we finalize the very simple wedding details, you should take this week to relax. Let Dylan show you around."

"But—"

"You can do as you choose, obviously," Haley said. "But Dylan really wants to do this, and honestly? This isn't like him, being so dead-set on anything. Not since he—" Haley blew out a breath. "I would consider it a huge favor if you went along. At least for today, if not the week."

Chelsea took stock of the other woman. A favor, huh? For her new employer? "Okay, then," she said, giving in. *Again.* This was becoming a habit where Dylan was concerned. "I guess I should get ready."

"Probably a good idea. He said he was on his way almost twenty—" She broke off at the unmistakable sound of a car door slamming shut. Another grin lit her face. "And that would be him now. He'll probably come in through the back, so—"

"Henry needs to get dressed. And he needs to eat something," Chelsea said, jumping to her feet. She wasn't prepared to see Dylan just yet. First she had to calm down and come up with a new strategy. Oh, and get rid of the damn butterflies that had decided to make her stomach their home. "And…um…I should change into something more appropriate for sightseeing."

"I can see why you might want to do just that," Haley said, laughter leaking into her voice. "Since we all know that jeans are so not appropriate for a casual day out. You know what? You should wear a short skirt, to show off your legs. Dylan's a sucker for long legs."

"That isn't what I meant!" Heat flooded Chelsea's cheeks at Haley's suggestion. Of course her jeans were fine. But her two-inch heeled boots were *not* fine for a day of walking. And she didn't care if Dylan was a sucker for long legs. Did not care at all. She was about to say those exact words—with emphasis—when heavy footsteps on the back porch put her in motion. "I'll be right back. After Henry is dressed and I change my shoes!"

She didn't wait for a response, just raced from the room and was halfway up the stairs before she stopped hearing Haley's not-smothered-at-all bouts of laughter. A second later, Dylan's deep voice greeting his sister reached Chelsea's ears. Forty-eight hours ago, she hadn't known a man like Dylan Foster existed.

And now, she had to spend the day—no, the *week*—with him.

A man her traitorous heart wanted to like, trust and get to know better. But why bother? Doing so would only be asking for trouble. Her wish to allow one trustworthy person into her life had been made in a desperate, lonely moment. In the cold light of day, she knew better. Because, even if she managed to push past her defenses to let Dylan in, even if she was wrong and he didn't view her as a helpless mess of a failure, what would be the point? She already knew the ending to that story, and she had no desire to be shown, yet again, that she was better off on her own.

Also troublesome, though on a smaller scale, was that Haley likely thought that she—due to Chelsea's odd behavior—was hot and bothered over Dylan. Who happened to be Haley's brother. And somehow, Chelsea was going to have to live and work with Haley. Resisting the urge to scream, Chelsea climbed the rest of the stairs and went to get Henry dressed.

Could this brand-new fresh start of hers get any more complicated?

God, she smelled good. Like orange blossoms and honey and something else, something flowery. Jasmine, maybe.

Whatever the combination, the result was a vibrant, evocative and entirely feminine scent that seemed perfectly suited for Chelsea.

She looked good, too. A little too good for Dylan's peace of mind. Her long dark hair was pulled away from her face in some sort of a clip, which he supposed served a practical purpose, but all it did for him was bring those gorgeous blue eyes of hers even more into focus.

If that wasn't enough, she'd chosen to wear black jeans that were neither too loose nor too tight, but somehow still managed to beautifully show off the long line of her legs. And then she'd topped it all off with a jade-green button-down shirt that looked soft to the touch and offered the tiniest glimpse of cleavage. It was as if she'd dressed with pleasing him in mind, because he'd always appreciated the leave-more-to-the-imagination casual look in the opposite sex than the show-every-inch-of-skin-possible type of ensembles.

And despite his attempts, he couldn't stop imagining. What her body looked like beneath those jeans and that soft-to-the-touch shirt. What her hair would look like tumbled around her face in disarray after she was kissed the way a woman should be kissed. Soundly. Passionately.

Fortunately, Henry's nonstop chatter in the backseat served well enough at keeping Dylan's mind from straying too far down that path. At the moment, the boy was asking his mother what had to be the hundredth *why* question since they'd left Haley's.

Okay, the fifth, but it felt as if he had a hundred more raring to go. So far, they'd covered "Why aren't there any more dinosaurs?", "Why do dogs bark and cats meow?", "Why does the red light mean stop and the green light mean go?" and Dylan's favorite—at this point, at least— "Why don't cows give root beer instead of milk?"

And one by one, Chelsea had answered each of her

son's questions with a mix of honesty and humor. From what he could see, she wasn't only a good mother, she was a patient and interested mother, which meant that Henry was one lucky little boy. The interaction also served to quell some of his concerns. A woman who was a good, patient and interested mother couldn't harbor too many dark secrets, could she?

Dylan eased his car to a stop at the light and listened to Chelsea's response to the newest question: "Why'd we come here for our brand-new fresh start instead of Disney World?"

Well. Looky there. Maybe he'd get some of *his* questions answered just by paying attention to Henry's.

"You know why, sweetie," Chelsea said. "I had a job here, not at Disney World. But wouldn't that be fun, living in such a place? If we were to move there, where would you want to live? One of the many castles or a pirate ship or…hmm, maybe—"

"A flying carpet!" Henry said. "So we could fly around and around and around. We could go anywhere we wanted, whenever we wanted!"

"True, but I'm not sure if living on a flying carpet is very realistic," Chelsea said, obviously trying not to laugh. "I mean, where would your bed go? And Teddy might be afraid of heights. I think we should live in a castle. If we ever move to Disney World, that is."

"That's 'cause you're a girl," Henry said in a poor-you sort of voice. "Where would you live, Dylan? I bet you wouldn't pick a boring castle."

"Pirate ship," Dylan said instantly. "We could still go anywhere we wanted, so long as there was water, and there would be plenty of room for a bed and your toys and Teddy."

"And cows who give you root beer instead of milk," Henry said. "Because if we're at Disney World, anything you wish can be true. Even that. Even boys who don't have daddies can have a daddy who will play with them. And…and…" Henry inhaled a shaky-sounding breath and stopped talking. A second later, two solid little-boy kicks hit the back of Dylan's seat.

And he had the sudden urge to pull over so he could turn around and see Henry's face. Reassure him, somehow. He didn't, though, because Henry wasn't his kid and however Chelsea chose to handle this was her call.

"Oh, honey." Chelsea unbuckled her seat belt and angled her body so she could look at Henry. "Not all boys have daddies. Not all girls, either. And lots of kids don't have mommies. And not all daddies and mommies play with their kids. But we have each other, right? And we're doing okay with just us, don't you think?"

"Yeah," the boy said. "I was just playing pretend. That's all."

Dylan eased off the car's brake and started forward, his thoughts on his own childhood and how fortunate he'd been to have two loving, involved parents. Due to Gavin and his history, and the camp he'd come to Steamboat Springs to start, Dylan had learned a lot about kids without parents and how that absence—without the proper, positive intervention—could negatively impact their entire lives. Chelsea was right. Too many children didn't have what Dylan and his siblings had grown up taking for granted.

"We can talk more about this later, if you'd like," Chelsea was saying to Henry. "If you have any new questions or…whatever you want."

"I know that." And then he said, "I love you, Mommy."

"Love you, too, sweetheart."

Chelsea buckled her seat belt and turned toward the passenger-side window, so Dylan couldn't see her face. He didn't know for sure, but he thought she was on the verge of tears. And that, along with the yearning he'd so plainly heard in Henry's voice, made him want to find the man who'd left his son fatherless and punch him square in the jaw. More than once.

Okay. Unfair. He didn't know what had happened. As far as he knew, Henry's father wasn't aware of the boy's existence. Or maybe—and this was a horrible thought— he'd died. Or hell, he could be in prison or…any one of a thousand other possibilities. None of them good. Some of them sad. Others—if true—would rest fully on Chelsea's shoulders.

He glanced her way before slowing for another stop. She still stared out the window, her spine ramrod straight, apparently lost in thought. Could she have purposely chosen to raise Henry without a father? Maybe. And, he supposed, there were plenty of damn good reasons a woman might make such a choice. But without knowing the details, it was stupid to speculate.

The facts were, for whatever reason, Henry's father wasn't around and the boy wanted a daddy to play with. Well. Dylan might not be Henry's father, but he could certainly give him a fun-filled morning instead of a general— and to a four-year-old boy, boring as all get-out—tour around Steamboat Springs. Dylan's initial thoughts were to show Chelsea and Henry some of the sights and, as the day progressed and appropriate moments presented themselves, pepper in a few questions. And hope she'd actually answer one or two.

He could still do that last part. He'd just skip the sightseeing in favor of an actual activity the kid would enjoy. As far as that went, he could plan activities with Henry in mind for the rest of the week. No harm there that Dylan could see. And while it wasn't his primary reason for changing course, doing so might even prove advantageous—make the boy happy and perhaps Chelsea would relax enough to open up about herself and her past.

And he had the perfect idea in mind.

Instead of going straight, as he'd planned, Dylan took a sharp right-hand turn and less than a mile later, another. The ice rink was directly ahead. "Don't know where any flying carpets are we can hitch a ride on, but how does ice-skating sound, Henry?"

"Ice-skating? I've never gone ice-skating before," the boy said, his voice regaining its normal level of excitement. "Can you teach me?"

"Oh yeah, I can definitely teach you. Once you learn how, ice-skating feels a lot like flying, because you can go super-duper fast."

"Did you hear that, Mommy?" Henry all but shouted. "We're going to fly on the ice today, and Dylan's gonna teach us how!"

Chelsea laughed and, after answering her son, said quietly to Dylan, "I'm sure this wasn't your original plan, but thank you. It's difficult to know how much to say when he talks about daddies. And…well, he'll love this. I will, too. You're rather adept at saving the day."

"No problem," Dylan said. "And if you're ever in the sharing mood, I'd like to hear about Henry's father." She didn't respond to that, naturally, and he didn't ask again. There would be more than enough time to revisit this topic. Later. After he taught a little boy how to fly.

Seeing as it was a Monday morning, there weren't many people at the ice rink. A small group of kids—probably around the same age as Henry—were in the middle of a class at one end of the rink, a young woman practiced a series of twirls and jumps in the center, and a few adults skated the length of the rink in a leisurely fashion.

Probably a good set of circumstances, as Chelsea hadn't skated in years. Not since she was a teenager, at least.

And, as Henry had said, he'd never skated before. Therefore, having plenty of room to practice staying upright meant little chance they'd fall smack in the path of another skater. But Chelsea sort of thought a few more people would be a bonus, as the presence of other bodies and voices would go a long way toward defusing the awkwardness that had started in the car when Henry had announced his daddy wish. She hated, and had since day one of Henry's life, that she couldn't provide her son with the oh-so-essential element of a father.

Of course, she was also intimately aware that having no father was far better than being crippled with a crappy father. Other than that ridiculous postcard, which hadn't even mentioned Henry, she hadn't seen or heard from Joel throughout Henry's entire existence, and even if she had, her doubts of his fathering ability were about as high as they could go. For both of these reasons, she had to believe that her son was better off in the long run.

Didn't stop her from wishing she could provide every last thing her son yearned for, including a man worthy of being his daddy. Sighing, she stood just off the ice and watched as Dylan slowly led Henry down the edge of the rink. Dylan skated backward, facing Henry, their hands entwined, while offering encouragement in a soft, patient voice. And Henry…God, her son was captivated, his attention entirely on Dylan and following his instructions.

To anyone else, the scene would look like a father teaching his son to skate. Even to Chelsea, it looked that way, and she knew the truth. But her son was glowing under Dylan's focused attention, and that caused her some concern. As much as she appreciated the time and consideration Dylan was giving Henry, it wouldn't last. How could it?

Dylan would eventually tire of playing fix-it to her problems—or she hoped he would, because she didn't like the idea that his goodwill was based solely on her less-than-ideal circumstances—and he'd go his way while she went hers. And where would that leave Henry then? She didn't know for sure, but clearly, the fallout wouldn't be good.

Henry had never had an attentive and caring male figure in his life, and if he was already bonding with Dylan, then the loss would cause a boatload of confusion. And pain. She'd rather be proactive now than try to pick up the pieces of her son's broken heart later.

Stepping cautiously onto the ice, she skated forward at a snail's pace until she'd made her way to Dylan and Henry. After sputtering to a stop beside them, she said, "How about giving Mommy a chance, sweetie? I'd like to skate with you, and I think I'm steady enough to keep us both from falling. Want to try?"

"Ah, not to be the bearer of bad news, but you're barely standing on your own," Dylan said, giving her a quick once-over. And, at the very second he did, her legs decided to wobble. She caught herself and he tossed her a teasing grin. "Based on that near fall, it looks as if Henry's in better skating shape. In fact, he's doing so well, I'd say he's a natural."

"Yeah, Mommy. I'm a natural!" Pulling one of his hands free from Dylan's, Henry raised it above his head as if he were about to go downhill on a roller coaster. "See? Besides that, he's teaching me how to fly, and I want to fly! Do you know how to fly?"

Well. He had her there. "Can't say that I do, but it might be fun to learn at the same time, don't you think?" Ugh. They were already several feet ahead of her. She inched forward again. "That way, once we both know what we're doing, we can fly together."

"Now, that *is* a grand idea," Dylan said as he carefully brought both himself and Henry to an easy, not-stumbling-at-all stop. "Let's try this. You two stand next to each other and hold hands, and I'll hold each of your other hands, and we'll skate around the rink together, as one."

"Oh. That wasn't precisely what I meant." Hold hands with Dylan? In the world of bad choices Chelsea could make right about now, that would have to top the list.

Well, okay, not the very top.

She could think of other, more intimate choices regarding Dylan that would easily take the first few slots. Kissing, as an example. Or…out of nowhere, an image filled her mind of a bare-chested Dylan pressing her tight against his body, his mouth on her neck and her hands on his back. Longing, swift and sure, curled in her belly and stretched through her limbs until every part of her felt hot. And bothered.

Oh, no. No, no, no. She was *not* hot and bothered over Dylan Foster. That image was due to her lack of…well, a sex life. It had been a long dry spell. Too long. Too dry. She was *not* fantasizing over Dylan, per se—it was just her body's natural need for fulfillment.

Lifting her chin, she went for cool indifference and said, "Thank you for the thought, but I was thinking that learning how to fly should be a mother-and-son experience. One of those once-in-a-lifetime moments. You can watch, though. And direct…from the sidelines."

"Problem is, I don't sit on the sidelines all that well," Dylan said, curiosity and interest lighting his gaze, his tone. Almost as if he'd stepped into her brain and had witnessed the imaginary scene for himself. "But if you'd rather that's what I do, I won't insist otherwise."

"Yes, I would rather—"

"I want to try it Dylan's way," Henry piped in. "Because he brought us here and he's…he's my friend." The boy tipped his head to look at Dylan. When he spoke, it was with innocent, unadulterated hope. "You are my friend, aren't you?"

And there went Chelsea's heart, straight to her toes. She wanted to leap in, to corral this moment in such a way to protect her son. In case Dylan didn't understand the significance of the question, of the yearning that fed it, and responded in too frivolous a manner. But she didn't. Couldn't, really. She was silenced by the expression on Dylan's face.

He looked…undone. As if whatever threads he held himself together with had all unraveled at once. Due to a question posed by a four-year-old. By *her* four-year-old.

"Henry," Dylan said, his voice harboring a plethora of emotion Chelsea couldn't begin to pull apart. Humility was in there, though. Along with…awe? "I would be most honored if we were friends."

"I don't know what that means." Henry's face scrunched into a mask of confusion and worry. "Does that mean you are my friend or you're not?"

Without any hesitation, Dylan knelt in front of Henry and grasped both of the boy's hands. "Yes, I am your friend. I hope that means you're my friend, as well? I could use someone like you on my side, you know. Good friends are hard to come by."

Henry nodded. "'Course I'm your friend. I have been since you stopped my mommy from crying. Only I didn't know if you were mine. Mommy says if you don't know something you should always ask, so I asked. And now I know." Then he looked at Chelsea and gave her that smile she loved so much. "Can we learn to fly now? Please?"

"Yes," she said, praying her voice didn't betray how close she was to tears. "We can learn to fly, and we'll do it Dylan's way. Since we're celebrating a new friendship."

Dylan rose to a stand and held out his right hand toward

her. Well, she couldn't refuse. Not now. So she swallowed away her nerves and put her hand in his. Skin touched skin and his warmth, his strength, bled into her in a slow, sure, satisfying sort of way that brought to mind carefree days spent soaking in the heat of the sun.

His eyes found hers, and there she saw another type of heat.

Uh-oh. She better be careful, because that look right there would unravel *her* threads. Every last one of them, kinks and knots and all.

"Ready for this?" he asked.

Unsure if she was imagining the double entendre, she answered the obvious meaning behind his question, and not the one simmering in her brain. In her heart. "For the ice-skating lesson?" She reached for Henry's hand with her free one and breathed in a head-clearing dose of oxygen. "Ready as I'll ever be," she all but chirped.

Heavens. What tiny forest animal had that voice originated from?

"Ready, Henry?" Dylan asked, apparently not noticing her odd vocal sounds.

"Ready, Freddy!" Henry said. "Let's fly!"

Laughing, Dylan positioned his body in front of them and, once he'd taken hold of Henry's other hand, skated backward at a leisurely pace. "We'll start off slow, but as soon as you two are steady on your feet, we'll go faster. I'll squeeze your hands when I'm about to speed up, so you'll be ready for it."

They skated the outskirts of the ice rink three full times before Dylan deemed they were ready to fly. He gripped her hand tighter, she assumed he did the same with Henry's, and she followed suit by firming her grasp on her son— though she wasn't altogether sure if hanging on to Henry for dear life helped him more than her. Didn't matter. They weren't going to fall.

She knew this in her gut. Dylan wouldn't let them lose control. Simple as that.

He gave her a delicious sort of wink, grinned at Henry and then looked over his shoulder to watch for oncoming traffic. Picking up speed slightly, he waited to be sure that Henry's and Chelsea's pace matched his and that all was good, and then he went a little faster. And he followed this pattern of speeding up, holding steady, speeding up and holding steady until they were, for all intents and purposes, flying around the rink.

A rush of excitement hit, and she laughed. Looked down at Henry, and the sight of his pink cheeks, huge smile and wide-open, don't-want-to-miss-a-thing eyes made her laugh again. This morning she'd enjoyed witnessing her son's carefree fun while he played with toys in his bedroom. Now she was experiencing that same emotion *with* him, not merely as a spectator.

Every ounce of apprehension, fear toward the future and pressure she carried on her shoulders, day in and day out, disappeared in the beauty of the moment. *This* was happiness.

And it was...glorious.

Chapter Eight

After ice-skating—or, as Henry was now calling it, ice flying—the three had stopped for a quick lunch before embarking on a shopping trip. Mostly of the window variety, but they'd gone into a few of the more interesting stores when their noses needed warming and, just a few minutes ago, a drugstore so Chelsea could buy minutes for her pay-as-you-go phone.

Now it was midafternoon, and Henry's legs were "squishy from flying" and he wanted to "rest them up" before walking in front of more windows. Dylan had laughingly agreed and, despite Chelsea's argument that they could just go home, had brought them here.

The Beanery was one of the city's most popular coffeehouses, and even in the middle of the afternoon, the place was near full capacity. Spying an empty table close to the entrance, Chelsea and Henry claimed it as theirs while Dylan waited in line to get their drinks.

Lola Parish, the owner of the Beanery and a close

friend of Dylan's mom, was behind the counter filling orders and chatting up a storm with her customers. She also happened to be his ex-wife's aunt. Elise was Lola's sister's daughter, the eldest of three girls, and for about a year after the divorce, Dylan had done his best to stay clear of the Beanery and its vivacious owner.

Those days were long past, though, and he'd stopped thinking of the connection between Lola and Elise ages ago.

Today, probably because of the comparisons—whether fair or not—he'd drawn between Chelsea and Elise, Dylan once again saw Elise when he looked at Lola. Idiotic for several reasons. The two women didn't resemble each other in the slightest. Lola was loud, brash—in the friendliest of manners—and unapologetic about both. She had flaming-red hair—a good deal redder than Dylan remembered from his younger days, so the brighter hue was probably courtesy of a bottle of dye—and tended to wear big, vibrant pieces of jewelry.

She was not an understated woman by any stretch of the imagination.

Elise, on the other hand, with her doe-like brown eyes, petite, slender physique and pale blonde hair, had embodied an unassuming, innocent facade. She spoke softly, sometimes so quietly one had to lean in to hear her, and she did not—seemingly, anyway—go to extremes to be noticed. But Dylan's attention had been captured, nonetheless.

As he got to know her, he'd learned the stark truth about her upbringing. Oh, he'd known her mother had died when Elise was in grade school, but he hadn't known about her father's overly strict rules and condemning nature, or his temper, or the strange household rules the girls had to follow. Elise had been desperate to get out of her father's house.

Loving Elise as he had, it had seemed the most expedient, if naive, solution was marriage. He'd proposed the same day they graduated from high school and they were married before the summer was over. His folks weren't thrilled with the idea, but once they saw his determination, they'd given him and Elise the support they needed.

Almost as soon as the vows were exchanged, she began to grow more distant. Secretive. At the time, he'd stupidly assumed she was worried about her younger sisters, Anna and Laurel, and feeling guilty for leaving them alone to deal with their dad. An assumption based on Elise's departures most evenings, with the explanation of spending time with her sisters.

And, okay, he couldn't say she hadn't felt any concern toward Anna and Laurel, but what he didn't know then was that for most of those evenings, she wasn't with them for more than an hour or two. She was too busy falling in love with another man and planning a different future. One that didn't include Dylan.

When too many discrepancies rose to the surface, she'd had the surprising decency to tell him face-to-face. Very quickly after that, well before Dylan could come up for air, she'd packed her bags, left and filed for divorce. Once the dust settled, Elise and her new family had left Steamboat Springs for some town in Maine that Dylan had never heard of, and to his knowledge, she hadn't returned to her home city since.

The only positive that had occurred from the whole friggin' mess was that Lola, after learning what was really going on in her late sister's household, had pushed for guardianship of her two underage nieces. Dylan didn't know all of the details, but soon after, Anna and Laurel had moved in with her and she'd finished the job of raising them.

So, no, there was no real reason to look at Lola and see

Elise, but today...the past felt much closer than it had in a long while. Well, he knew why, and he'd deal with it.

"Hey there, Dylan," Lola said, cutting into his thoughts.

"Hi, Lola." Dylan gave himself a swift mental shake. "Busy as usual, I see."

"That we are, and pleased about it, as well. How are you doing today?" Lola's long, dangly earrings—a row of miniature coffee mugs connected by the handles in various bright shades—bobbed as she talked. "And what can I get for you?"

"Doing well. Thanks for asking," Dylan said. "Ah...I need a hot chocolate, a caramel latte and a black coffee, along with two of your cinnamon rolls and—" Dylan looked over the selection of baked goods and tried to guess what Henry would like "—a snickerdoodle cookie."

"Snickerdoodles are always a good choice for a growing boy." Lola nodded toward the table where Chelsea and Henry sat. "You used to love them, if I recall correctly."

"Did and still do." The easy back-and-forth helped relax his tension. This was Lola. Almost a second mom to all the Foster kids. "But come on, your cinnamon rolls are legendary."

Chuckling, Lola started to prepare his order. They chatted some as she did, about the weather, the upcoming summer season and how fast Reid's babies were changing.

Then she might as well have conked him in the head with a whiskey bottle, because she said, "Did your mom mention that one of my chicks is returning to the nest soon? She'll be staying with me until she gets settled."

"Elise? She's...ah, that is—"

"Oh, heavens. I'm sorry, Dylan." Lola shook her head as if chastising herself. She loaded a tray with the drinks and snacks. "Sometimes I forget...but no, I'm speaking of Anna. Not Elise. I rarely talk to her these days. Usually only at the holidays."

"Gotcha. I'm sure having Anna home will be nice."

"It sure will." Lola accepted his credit card and ran it through. "Enjoy," she said, returning the card and pushing the tray toward him. "And I'm sorry if you thought—"

"No worries. All's good." He picked up the tray. "Thanks, Lola. Hope to see you soon."

He headed toward the table, his eyes on Chelsea and Henry. Relief that it was the middle Rockwood sister coming home hadn't yet overtaken his shock at believing, even for a second, that his ex-wife was readying herself to move back to Steamboat Springs. On the good-news front, he hadn't felt a flicker of panic or anger at the possibility. Only shock.

That seemed a reasonable reaction for a man to have in such a circumstance. Rational.

But his little jaunt down memory lane while waiting in line reinforced his decision to learn what he could about Chelsea, ascertain she didn't have damaging secrets or a hidden agenda or... Hell. Dylan paused midstride.

What was so wrong with admitting he liked the woman and her son? Not a damn thing, that was what. Perhaps once he confirmed she was exactly the person she'd presented herself as—a single mom who'd faced some struggles and was now trying to create a better life for her and her son—he'd consider the possibility of more. If, of course, she was interested in the like.

Based on their interaction at the ice rink, he thought she might be.

He walked the final few steps to the table and set down the tray, gave a second's thought of who he should sit next to and slid in beside Henry. Better to be able to see Chelsea's eyes as they talked, and honestly, sitting that close would likely muck with his ability to think.

"Hope you're a fan of snickerdoodle cookies, Henry, because that's what I got you," Dylan said. "And for you, my lady," he said to Chelsea, "the latte you requested and the best cinnamon roll you'll ever taste. Guaranteed."

"What do I get if you're wrong and this isn't the best cinnamon roll I've ever tasted?" she asked. "I hope it's something good, because my grandmother's recipe for cinnamon rolls? Those are the best."

"People come here just for the cinnamon rolls, so that seems doubtful. But if such a miracle were to happen?" Dylan scratched his head, as if mulling over her question. "I know. What if you tell me *any* one thing about you, from before we met?"

"Be more specific," Chelsea said. "How long before?"

"I don't care," he said. "Whenever you want. Could be from when you were a kid or the minute before you walked into Foster's or any moment in between. Totally your call."

"Anything I want?"

"Anything at all."

"That's easy enough, so sure. Any one thing." She picked up the cinnamon roll and brought it to her mouth, stopped and narrowed her eyes. "You're going to believe me about which is better, though, right? I don't have to bake a batch for you to test?"

"I expect you'll be honest, but if you feel the womanly need to bake something as special as your grandmother's cinnamon rolls for me, I certainly won't object." He downed a mouthful of coffee. "Or apple pie. I'm a sucker for apple pie."

Arching a brow, she honed in on his sole questionable phrase. "Did you really just say *womanly need*?"

He shrugged, grinned. "We all have needs. Who am I to condemn yours?"

She wrinkled her nose in confused amusement. It was a look, Dylan decided, that took her straight past cute all the way to adorable. "I'll just taste this cinnamon roll now and we can move on to another topic of discussion. One that does not include womanly needs."

"Sure," he said easily. "Though, if you decide to circle back around, I'm not opposed to a conversation about womanly needs. I'll talk about whatever you want."

"Uh-huh." She took a large bite of the pastry, chewing it slowly, her tongue darting out to lick the crumbs off her lips, and Dylan was…transfixed.

He could almost imagine the feel, the taste of her lips right now. They would be soft and warm, coated in a delectable mix of sweetness and spice. Dylan closed his eyes and let out a ragged breath, tried to cool the heat simmering in his blood. Cripes. Since when did a woman involved in the simple act of eating ramp up his desire?

"Well, I can see why everyone loves these cinnamon rolls," Chelsea said, her voice also sweet. Also spicy. Lord help him. "And this is hard to admit, but I can't definitively declare my grandmother's recipe tops this one. It's a close call."

"Ah, I see what you're doing. This way, you don't have to admit Lola's the winner, which means you don't have to spill any of your secrets."

She snorted and rolled her eyes at Henry, who giggled in response. The boy had listened to the conversation while drinking his cocoa and eating his cookie without uttering so much as a syllable. Dylan had started to worry if the kid was okay. Based on that giggle, he was fine.

"It would be a nice way to divert, if that's what I was doing." Chelsea broke off a chunk of the pastry and popped the piece into her mouth, and he came darn close to groaning out loud. Fortunately—for his sanity and the easing-into-uncomfortable fit of his jeans—her tongue stayed put. "I honestly can't say if one is better than the other. I might have to try them side by side."

"Fair enough." Dylan drummed his fingers against the

surface of the table. "But is there any way I can convince you to share one thing from your past anyhow?"

She fidgeted in her seat. "That wasn't the deal we made."

"You can't blame a guy for being curious." Most folks naturally talked about their lives. Little things here and there, but so far—unless she was conversing with Henry about a topic he'd brought up—Chelsea didn't say much. Deciding to try to lead her into a discussion using a subject *she'd* already broached, he asked, "What was your grandmother's name?"

"Sophia. She was…amazing."

"I never knew her," Henry said, finding his voice. "She went to heaven before I was born but Mommy says she was really nice."

"I'm sure she was," Dylan said. "And I'm sorry you didn't get to meet her."

"Me, too. Mommy says she watches us from the clouds to see if we're happy." Then, with a more-intelligent-than-his-age gleam in his eyes, Henry said, "She prolly saw the night I was born, when it was just me and Mommy and no one else. That was a happy night."

"Yes, sweetie. Very, very happy."

"But we were sad when the firemen came and watered the apartment so the fire wouldn't burn it to the ground." He stopped and inhaled a breath. "And when Uncle Kirk threw our clothes from the window for you to catch, he was all mad and…and…yelling. Even though you said it was just a pickup game. Did Great-grandma watch when that stuff happened, too?"

In a strangled-sounding voice, Chelsea said, "I'd like to think Sophia is always watching us, even in the not-so-great moments. Why all these questions, Henry?"

"Because I wondered if Great-grandma sees everything we do or if she only sees some of the stuff we do." Small shoulders lifted in a slight shrug. "Also, Dylan wanted to know stories about us and I thought of those ones first. Oh! I thought of another one! What about when—"

"Stop, Henry." Chelsea didn't speak loudly or forcefully, but her entire body was still, almost frozen, and Dylan heard the tremor shaking those two measly words clear as day. Was she afraid of whatever tale Henry was about to detail next? "Some stories are better left private."

"Oh, right. What about the Teddy story? I wanted to tell Dylan about how he was yours when you were a little girl and you saved him for your whole life just for me."

"I think that's a great story to share with Dylan." Chelsea blinked several times in quick succession, as if trying to keep her emotions under control. "Because even when I was a little girl, I knew that someday I'd have the most wonderful, funny, amazing son ever, and that sometimes he'd need a buddy to keep him company, like I did. So I took very, very good care of Teddy and saved him for you."

"Because you don't need him anymore, right? You have me."

"That's right."

"But what about when I grow all up and go away?"

"Well, I think that's something you shouldn't worry about," Chelsea said quietly. "I'd rather you think about what makes you happy. Okay?"

"And if I 'cide something would make me happy that I don't have, then what?" Henry dropped his gaze to his hands, which were holding his almost-empty cup of cocoa.

"Then, so long as what you want won't hurt someone else, you should do your best to get it. And if you let me in on what will make you happy, I can help you." Chelsea reached across the table and stroked her son's arm. "That's what moms are for, kiddo."

Throughout the mother-and-son exchange, Dylan had listened with curiosity and interest—and yeah, quite a lot of annoyance toward Uncle Kirk—but he'd held his tongue. What they discussed seemed too serious, private and personal for him to interrupt. And as he'd listened, his heart took a rather substantial lead over his brain.

Because, dammit all, Dylan was beginning to think that Gavin had been right yesterday morning and that he did want more in his life than he currently had. Something of…meaning.

And he had a sneaking suspicion that what he wanted, what would make him the most content, were the two people sitting at this table with him. He'd even had the ridiculous thought that he'd like to give them many happy moments for Grandmother Sophia to watch from the clouds. Dylan didn't understand how any of those thoughts were possible.

He wasn't his sister, who swore up and down and side to side that her heart had recognized Gavin almost instantly. And he wasn't his brothers, who'd all but moved heaven and earth in the name of love, while knowing full well the heartache that awaited them if they failed.

No. He was not his siblings.

But he just might have a helluva lot more in common with them than he'd thought. A prospect that did not sit well with him. Ever since his marriage to Elise, he'd preferred sane, rational, predictable behavior. He preferred analyzing the lay of the land before taking so much as a solitary step in a different, uncharted direction. And he did not go for spontaneous gestures or letting his emotions dictate his behavior.

Until Chelsea and Henry, these *rules* of his had done the trick. But this woman and her child made him want to shed his hardened skin and revert to his prior self. And the merest possibility of giving in to that temptation seemed, at once, compelling and terrifying.

So what was he supposed to do?

With a sharp inhale, he weighed the almighty logic against the inane but also powerful instinct raging inside. Chelsea and Henry were not his to claim, even if his heart demanded he find a way to do just that, no matter how long it might take. His brain, however, wouldn't allow him to abandon everything he'd learned to go freely down that path. Yet after today, he had a hunch that he'd drive himself ten kinds of crazy if he tried to fully ignore either his brain or his heart in favor of the other. One was too adamant, the other too ingrained.

So he supposed he'd have to skirt the middle. Stay open enough to see where this instinct of his took him while keeping just enough distance to ensure he didn't fall too hard, too fast, only to end up kicking himself for making the same mistake twice.

Fine. He'd bend a little. He'd allow the opportunity for something good—something *more* and *meaningful*—to occur, but on his terms. The very second he recognized a problem that couldn't be logically explained and then dismissed, he'd put the kibosh on the whole damn deal and return to telling his heart to butt out and leave him alone.

One chance. That was all he had in him. Just one.

"'Night, Henry. Sleep tight." Chelsea kissed her son on his forehead, tucked his blankets in around his body and handed him a flashlight. "Say hi to the love bugs for me."

"I don't want those love bugs. You can have them!"

"Oh, the love bugs are all for you!" She tickled him until he laughed and then made her way to the door. Right before switching off the light, she said, "Don't stay up too late playing shadow puppets. Dylan will be here in the morning."

She'd tried—oh, how she'd tried—to get out of their spending a second day with him, but in the end, she'd failed. Dylan's insistence combined with Henry's enthusiasm over the idea had won out. And honestly, she couldn't claim that the hours spent together had been awful.

She'd enjoyed herself. Far more than she'd expected, but her concerns over Henry bonding too quickly, too tightly with a man who had no reason to stick around hadn't abated. Without asking, she already knew that Henry was smitten, and she could probably guess why.

Her little boy was likely seeing Dylan as a daddy figure, and she had no clue how to handle such a situation without hurting Henry. If she refused to let him spend time with Dylan, he'd be hurt and sad and confused. If she let this continue and Dylan let Henry down, her son would still be hurt and sad and confused. The only good outcome was if Dylan remained a positive presence in Henry's life, and the possibility of that seemed unlikely.

Releasing a sigh, she closed Henry's door and went to her bedroom. Before visiting with Gavin and Haley, she needed to call her sister. Lindsay had the address for the house Chelsea had thought she'd be living in for the next many months, and while her sister didn't send letters often, she just might decide to do so.

Lindsay remained the one family member Chelsea had any contact with. Her relationship with her parents was nonexistent, and no, she couldn't claim to like them, but she would want to know if something happened to them. Four years later, and she was still shocked, still hurt, that they'd decided to disown her because she wouldn't let them raise *her* son.

It remained just as ridiculous today as it was then.

Sitting on the edge of the bed, Chelsea dialed her sister's phone number and mentally crossed her fingers that she wouldn't have to talk to Kirk. She didn't, as it was her sister who answered on the second ring. "Is this a good time for you?" she asked.

"It's fine," Lindsay said. "Kirk is in the shower, and even if he wasn't, I'm allowed to talk to my sister. I know he hasn't always been kind to you, but he isn't a monster."

"Not a monster, no." Monsterish enough, so far as Chelsea was concerned, with his needy, immature and controlling behavior. She didn't say any of those things, of course, as she had before. To deaf ears. Brightening her voice, she said, "We're here, but our circumstances have changed. Let me give you our new address."

The sisters chatted about Steamboat Springs and Chelsea's job, but not for too long. It was nice, though, hearing her sister's voice and maintaining their connection, as slim as it was. After promising she'd call again in a few weeks, Chelsea hung up.

She had yet to decide if Lindsay truly didn't see her husband as he was or if she refused to admit so aloud, because if she did, she'd then have to do something about it. Strange, how they'd both grown up in the same household and yet saw the world around them so differently.

Well. Lindsay had been closer to their parents' ideal than Chelsea. That could be part of the reason. And, if she were to be honest, once upon a time, they weren't quite so different.

Joel was partially cut from the same cloth as Kirk, as her father. Not the yelling, controlling portion, but the selfish life-is-all-about-me portion. And while Chelsea hadn't recognized the depth of his self-involvement when she was embroiled in their relationship, she eventually had. Maybe all Lindsay needed was more time to get to the same place Chelsea had.

It was a hopeful thought. And one Chelsea prayed would come to pass, but after many attempts to get through to her sister, she'd realized that Lindsay's life wasn't her responsibility. There was only so much she could do. She'd be there for her, if and when Lindsay reached out. Until then, Chelsea had more than enough on her plate to worry about.

Such as the man she had to spend tomorrow with. The same man, who, due to a little boy's words, had completely come undone in front of her today.

Chapter Nine

"Where are we going, Dylan?" Henry asked from the backseat of Dylan's car on Saturday morning. Chelsea was surprised he'd waited this long, as they'd already been on the road for close to ten minutes. "I bet it will be somewhere fun!"

"You bet, huh?" Chelsea said, pivoting slightly in her seat so she could see her son. "Maybe not. Maybe we're headed to the mall so we can shop for clothes. For you!"

Henry scowled for about two seconds before giving his head a decisive shake. "Uh-uh, and no way! I don't want to do that and Dylan won't want to, either!"

Dylan chuckled while he drove. "Well," he said, "I did have other plans for us, but if your mom thinks you need clothes, I don't mind changing them."

Chelsea winked at Henry to let him in on the joke.

"You guys are silly and I don't believe you at all!" he said, laughing. "Tell me where we're going, Dylan. Pretty please? Ice flying again? Or the movies? Or something new?"

"Something new, but it's a surprise. And on a different scale than anything else we've done this week. Overall, it…ah…should be enjoyable." He then lowered his voice, making it seem as if he were mumbling to himself, and said, "I hope so, anyway."

"Mommy? Tell me!"

"I don't know, sweetie. I have no idea what's on Dylan's agenda."

But if she had to guess, she would assume the same as Henry—somewhere fun. For the past five days, Dylan had hit it out of the ballpark with one childcentric activity after another. She'd tried to dissuade him on Tuesday and Wednesday, but by Thursday she'd stopped fighting so hard. For Henry's sake. This might be the only experience he would ever have that would remotely resemble a father-son type of relationship.

Even with her concerns—all valid and sensible—she couldn't bring herself to yank the rug out from under Henry's feet. Not yet. Not unless she had no choice.

"You really don't know?" Henry asked, his doubt ringing loud and clear.

"No, baby, I really don't." Facing front again, Chelsea tried to think about anything other than how ridiculously sexy Dylan looked in his plain, not-fancy-at-all long-sleeved charcoal-gray thermal jersey and so-dark-they-were-almost-black gray denim jeans. It wasn't the clothes so much as the man himself. He just had that strong, capable, all-male look going for him.

She was finding it increasingly difficult not to pay attention to the details of his body. It was both annoying and liberating. Annoying because she didn't want Dylan to have such an effect on her. Liberating because…well, her entire focus had been on Henry and making ends meet for so long, she'd—somewhere along the way—forgotten what it felt like to be a girl.

As in a spray-on-perfume, shave-her-legs, do-her-nails, primp-and-feel-good-about-how-she-looked girl. Oh, she always took care with her appearance, but she hadn't *really* cared. She'd gone through the motions. But this week, she'd suddenly started caring again.

That didn't mean she appreciated her intense reaction to Dylan. Or how she seemed to pick up on something different every time she so much as glanced in his direction.

Like the way the sun turned his hair from a warm medium brown to a lustrous mix of coppery shades. Or how his eyes would go from green to brown to somewhere in between in the snap of a finger, depending on the conversation, the lighting or, she guessed, his mood. Or how when he became focused on one thing or another that muscle in his jaw would start twitching. That twitch had just about hypnotized her more than once already.

Long, strong legs. A firm set of shoulders. Narrow hips and a trim waist. Oh, but his hands... She might love the look of his hands the most. Also strong. Also capable. And perfect for any number of uses. Mixing drinks, obviously. But she imagined those hands would be equally as adept at cutting down a tree or, on the opposite end of the spectrum, playing with a puppy.

Or...eliciting moans of passion, of pleas for more, from a woman. From her.

Forcing her thoughts to return to reality, she visualized a cold bucket of water drenching her clear to the skin. Not as good as an actual bucket of cold water, but it worked well enough.

When she'd regained some semblance of normalcy, she asked Dylan quietly, "Okay, you can tell me. Where are we going?"

"I suppose I could, but I'm not going to," Dylan said with a sidelong grin. "Be patient. We'll be there soon enough, and then I'll let you in on how we're spending the next few hours."

"You aren't going to buy something expensive that you think I need, are you?" She was mostly joking, but not all the way. She hadn't quite decided why Dylan was spending so much of his time with her and Henry. "Like a car or…a present for Henry?"

He laughed. A robust, rich, warm sound of pleasure. Great. Just another piece of the freaking Dylan Foster puzzle for her to fantasize about, because that laugh? Amazing. Sexy. Beautiful. Which, in Chelsea's mind, also equaled annoying.

"No," he said after he managed to squelch his laughter. "My plan for the day is not buying you a car, but I wonder…would you accept if I did?"

"Only if it came with a trunk that was loaded with diamonds and gold nuggets," she quipped. "And even then, I wouldn't want or need the car. Just the loot."

"Diamonds are for girls to get married with," Henry said, showing how often he paid attention, even when he was quiet. "Haley showed me her 'gagement ring from Gavin and told me that he gave it to her in a big balloon in the sky. 'Cause he wanted her to marry him, but I didn't see any gold nuggets."

"Haley has a beautiful ring, and I'm glad she told you that story." Absently, Chelsea rubbed her ring finger. She'd never had an engagement ring. She'd never had a man love her enough to want to propose. Which was fine. Perfectly fine, even.

"Do all 'gagement rings have to have diamonds?" Henry asked. "And is it always the boy who asks the girl to be married? And how did Gavin take Haley in a big balloon in the sky? Where did they sit? And how big of a balloon was it? And—"

"Lots of engagement rings have diamonds," Chelsea said before Henry could ask ten more questions she wouldn't remember by the time she answered the first set. "But not all of them do, and they can have any type of gem or no gems at all. The man usually asks the woman to get married, but the woman can ask, too. It's about knowing you love the other person and deciding that you want to be their family, and that you want them to be yours." She pulled in a breath. What else? Oh. "And I'm guessing the big balloon in the sky was a hot-air balloon. They're really, really big. And they have a basket under the balloon that people stand in."

"And they go up high in the sky? Like with the clouds?"

"Yes, they do."

"If we went in one, would we be able to see Great-grandma watching us?"

Oh. Jeez. How to answer? "Sweetie, we wouldn't be able to see her, but we might be able to feel her love. We can do that from the ground, too."

"So she can't ever really be a part of our family, can she?"

Chelsea swallowed past the lump in her throat and pressed her fingertips to her cheeks, trying to stop the tears that were building behind her eyes. Her son yearned for more of a family than just the two of them. She understood. Her heart ached with how well she understood.

"Not in the way we'd like, sweetie, no." Dammit. Her voice sounded thick, heavy with emotion. "But…that's why I talk about her so much. I miss her. And I know she would have loved to have really known you. She… would've taught you to bake, just like she taught me."

It was her grandmother Sophia who'd given her Teddy. It was Sophia who'd stood up to Chelsea's father and told him he was a bully, with the way he yelled and criticized his children. Sophia had been her ally. She'd died when

Chelsea was in junior high school, and not a single day had passed since that she hadn't thought of her.

"I think that's sad, Mommy," Henry said. "And not fair at all."

"I agree. It is sad, and no, it isn't fair when we lose the people we love." Wiping her eyes again, Chelsea tried to think of something happy and bright and beautiful. All that was in her mind, though, was Sophia. "I'm sorry, Henry. I wish you could've known her."

Her son didn't respond, and Chelsea stared out the window. Hopefully, whatever Dylan had planned would lift Henry's spirits.

"Tell me about Sophia," Dylan said softly. "Introduce her to me."

"What do you mean, introduce her to you?"

"If you were bringing her to my house to meet me, what would I need to know?"

"Oh. Well, I'd tell you to have gingersnap cookies on hand, because they were one of her favorite treats. The boxed ones, mind you."

"Wait a minute. Your amazing baker of a grandmother preferred boxed cookies to baking them herself?" Dylan slowed at a corner and turned into a residential neighborhood. "That's kind of funny. And endearing."

"Only gingersnaps, but yes. She used to keep a box under her bed, so if she woke up at night hungry she wouldn't have to go to the kitchen." Chelsea sighed, remembering sleepovers where she and Sophia had sat in bed and munched on cookies, talking. And how Sophia would promise her that someday she wouldn't be so unhappy. That someday she'd be able to move out of her parents' house and wouldn't have to deal with her dad's anger issues ever again.

Dylan slowed down and pulled into the driveway of a blue-and-white-painted gingerbread-style house. Fitting, with all the talk about Sophia's gingersnaps, and Chelsea thought the house was lovely. She just couldn't imagine what they were doing here. Maybe a friend of Dylan's had children around Henry's age and this was a playdate of sorts?

"Before you ask, this is Reid and Daisy's home." Dylan turned off the ignition and pocketed his keys. "And—don't get mad at me—but we're here to babysit. Reid mentioned that he wanted to give Daisy a break. I volunteered our services." He flashed her a sweet-as-pie grin. "You don't mind, do you?"

"No, of course not. But you're sure Reid and Daisy are okay with me helping? And Henry hasn't spent much time with babies."

"Pretty sure Reid and Daisy trust me enough to know I wouldn't bring someone into their home they'd have an issue with, and I've thought of Henry." Swiveling in his seat to look at Henry, Dylan said, "Daisy has a couple of nieces who come over all the time, so they have toys. And they have a slide and a swing set in their backyard. Think you'll have fun?"

"Prolly," Henry said. "But what if I want to play with the babies?"

"They're still too little to really play with," Dylan said. "But you can talk to them, and they seem to like to smile a lot, and they're awfully cute when they do."

"Okay," Henry said, happy with the prospect. "Let's do it!"

Chelsea opened her door, ready to set Henry free from his safety seat, when Dylan leaned in close—so close she could smell the clean scent of the shampoo he'd used that morning—and said, "Your son rocks."

Such a simple statement, but pleasure that someone else—that *Dylan*—had noticed the awesomeness of her son made her smile. "He was born that way. Seriously."

"Ah…maybe," Dylan said, his breath tickling her ear. And just like the touch of his hand on hers the other day, a feeling of warmth, of satisfaction, poured into her. "But I think you can claim a large portion of the credit. And I think you should. Don't sell yourself short, Chelsea."

"I…um… Thank you." If she moved her head ever so slightly, his lips would be right there, in kissable range. Another saturating wash of warmth coated her skin, born from embarrassment and maybe some shyness at the concept. Anticipation lived there, too, and she had the thought that if Henry wasn't in the backseat, she might go for it. Just to see who would kiss whom. "We should go," she said. "Before your brother wonders what we're doing."

"Oh, I'm guessing he'd be able to figure that one out."

Chelsea's butterflies returned with a vengeance and her skin tingled with desire. Did that mean Dylan's thoughts had mirrored hers? Or was she reading too much into his words?

The latter, probably, since the reason he'd leaned in so close was to praise Henry and not to tell her she looked beautiful or that he hadn't been able to stop thinking about her or…well, any other wooing type of compliment. He liked her son, and that was that.

Within a matter of minutes, the three were walking toward the house's entrance. The door swung open, and the same red-haired woman Chelsea had seen in the photograph on Haley's mantel stood there with one of the babies in her arms.

"You are an angel," she said to Dylan. "And you've brought two more angels with you. Thank you for doing this today."

"Welcome, Daisy," Dylan said, reaching the porch. He gave her a chaste, brotherly kiss on her cheek. "And in case you haven't figured it out, this bouncy boy right here is Henry, and this—" he nodded toward Chelsea "—is his mother, Chelsea."

"Nice to meet you guys. Come on in." She stepped back so everyone could enter. "Reid is changing Alexander, and I just changed Charlotte. Both are fed and should be tired enough to go down for naps soon. If you're lucky, they'll sleep most of the time we're gone."

Chelsea smiled. "I wouldn't mind if they stayed awake."

"Shh. Be careful what you wish for," Daisy said with a gentle laugh. "Or be more specific. One at a time is easy enough, but when they both get going...it can get chaotic fast."

Daisy led them into the living room, which was painted a deep ocean blue. The shade was dark enough to avoid the description of *vivid*, while still emanating warmth and richness. That, along with the medium earthy-brown hue coating the baseboards and crown molding, gave the space a tranquil, stylish air. However, the sturdy, simple furnishings—the wood-framed sofa and chairs with plump, colorful cushions, the extralarge flat-screen television, unique decorative accents and, naturally, various baby paraphernalia, including two baby swings—added coziness and livability. It was, Chelsea thought, a room to relax in.

Henry beelined for the small crate of toys he'd spied sitting on top of the coffee table, skidded to a stop and glanced at Daisy. "Can I play with these toys?" he asked, pleasing Chelsea with his manners. He didn't always remember. "Or are they only for the babies?"

"Of course you can play with them." Daisy sat down on the sofa, Charlotte still in her arms. The baby didn't look sleepy at all. She was too intrigued by the activity and new voices. "We brought them down from the extra bedroom for that exact reason."

That was all it took. Henry knelt in front of the coffee

table and started removing each of the toys one by one in order to decide which he wanted to play with first. Chelsea figured he'd be well occupied for a good hour. Maybe more.

"You two are making me nervous," Daisy said. She patted the cushion next to her and looked at Chelsea. "Please sit down and make yourself comfortable. Reid shouldn't be long."

Dylan took one of the chairs and Chelsea, following Daisy's lead, sat beside her on the sofa. Charlotte cooed at her and then graced her with a big, gummy smile. "Oh, she's gorgeous. And so sweet," she said to Daisy. "Though I'm sure you hear that all the time."

Chuckling, Dylan and Daisy exchanged a look. "Charlotte is gorgeous," he said. "No question there, and she can be very sweet. She can also be…rather loud and I expect as she grows, she'll have the same determined, stubborn-as-a-mule streak that Haley has."

"He isn't wrong," Daisy said, kissing Charlotte on the top of her head. "This one has a set of lungs on her you wouldn't believe, while Alex tends to be the quiet-as-a-mouse twin."

"That's because our daughter makes enough noise for both of them," Reid said as he entered the room with Alex propped on his hip. "And however she turns out is fine with me, even if she does become a stubborn, willful carbon copy of her aunt Haley."

"I'd rather that she be stubborn," said Daisy, "than afraid to go for what she wants."

"I agree wholeheartedly," Chelsea said. "Better to take risks than…" She stopped. Breathed. Did she really believe it was better to put yourself on the line for something you wanted than it was to exist in a safe, if not ideal, world?

For Henry, yes. Without a doubt. For herself? She didn't know.

"Settle for half of a life?" Reid filled the silence and saved her from an awkward moment. He positioned Alexander on his lap so the baby was sitting against his chest for support, and then swung his other arm over Daisy's shoulders. "That's the only way to do it, in my opinion. Some risks are necessary. In fact…"

Reid went on to share how he'd planned his wedding to Daisy, from beginning to end—venue, decorations, food, *all* of it—even though she'd repeatedly refused his proposal. As he continued speaking, Dylan's jaw hardened and Chelsea guessed that muscle was twitching away— she just wasn't close enough to verify—and his eyes sort of glazed over, as if he'd become lost in thought. Or perhaps he'd just heard the story so many times he'd zoned off.

"Fortunately," Reid said, finishing the tale, "she showed up *almost* on time, having driven to California and back in less than twenty-four hours." He grinned at his wife. "I heard that ornery dog of hers first, and bam, there was Daisy. A little wrinkled, but beautiful."

Huh. Chelsea could not fathom such a show of love or having such strength of hope to go to those lengths. "That's remarkable," she said. "I'm glad for the happy ending."

Henry had stopped playing with his toys to listen to the story as well, and she prepped herself for more of his rapid-fire question sessions. Surprisingly, he kept quiet.

"Where is Jinx?" Dylan asked, awakening from his coma. "She's usually attached to my legs by now, begging for attention."

"Pouting from being scolded," Daisy said softly, as Charlotte's eyes were heavy and starting to close. "You know how Jinx thinks she's the mother of these babies, right? Well, she chewed one of the legs on Charlotte's crib this morning when I was in the middle of changing Alex. Reid was in the shower. I think my beloved whippet was trying to eat her way through the crib to care for Charlotte herself." Daisy trailed a finger down the side of Charlotte's face. "I'm sure once Jinx stops pouting, she'll run down here to visit. Probably after we leave."

"Which we should do soon," Reid said. "But before we take off, tell us more about you, Chelsea. We hardly had time to talk the other day at the restaurant. Dylan says you came to Steamboat Springs for a job that fell through?"

"Yes, a house-sitting job," she said. "Unfortunately, we had a late start and my phone was out of minutes. When the owners weren't able to contact me, they filled the position with someone else." Chelsea inwardly cringed. Lord, that made her seem irresponsible and unorganized. "I guess you could call it a comedy of errors on my part. I didn't know I'd lost the position until after we'd arrived. By then, it seemed…um, more financially viable to stay put."

"And then your car broke down," Daisy said. "That must have been awful. And terrifying. I'm so sorry you had such a poor welcome to Steamboat Springs."

"It's been a more difficult transition than I'd anticipated," she said, "but honestly, it would have been a lot more difficult without Dylan and everyone else's help. The entire Foster family has been…well, wonderful. Meeting Dylan was a stroke of good fortune and I'm just…um… very grateful."

Wow. She hadn't meant to say quite that much, but her words were true and heartfelt. Without Dylan, she wasn't sure where she and Henry would be now. Probably stuck in a miserable motel, surviving on peanut butter and crackers.

Dylan gave her an odd, inscrutable look and cleared

his throat. Standing, he said, "Okay, you two need to get going. I know the drill, and I'll show Chelsea where everything is."

Reid passed Alex to Dylan before helping his wife to stand. "Want to put her in the crib yourself?" he asked, referring to the now fast-asleep Charlotte.

Daisy nodded and softly stepped from the room. Once she was gone, Reid motioned to a video baby monitor on an end table, saying, "There's another in the kitchen."

"Get your wife and get out of here," Dylan said again with some humor. He wasn't looking at Reid, though. He was making silly grins at Alexander, who was happily babbling in return. "Yeah, you know you're adorable, don't you?"

And the look of this strong, capable, all-male, *sexy* man cuddling his infant nephew with such sweet devotion melted Chelsea's heart to mush. Yes, Alexander was indeed adorable. But Uncle Dylan was pretty darn adorable, too.

A minute later, Daisy returned. She kissed Alexander on the cheek and then curled her arm into Reid's, saying, "We should go before someone starts crying and I feel guilty all over again. You'll never get me out of here if that happens."

"What's there to feel guilty about?" Dylan said. "One baby is asleep. The other is content to be drooling all over my shirt. So have fun and don't worry. We'll be fine."

Everything was absolutely *not* fine.

Within thirty minutes of Reid and Daisy's departure, Chelsea and Dylan were up to their eyeballs in chaos. Both babies were crying at the top of their lungs, Jinx was whining almost as loudly because the dog wanted the grown-ups to make *her* babies happy and Henry was relentlessly begging his mother—whom he'd never before had to share with another child, let alone a crying infant—to play with him...*now*.

"Henry, honey," Chelsea said as she paced the twins' nursery with Charlotte in her arms. "I know you're frustrated, and as soon as I can calm Charlotte, we'll do something together. But right now, I need you to be patient and understanding."

Dylan and Alexander were in the rocking chair, which generally worked wonders at soothing his nephew's fussy periods, but not today. For reasons unknown to him, Alex was screaming bloody murder. He didn't want a bottle. He didn't need to be changed. He didn't have a fever. He was just...ticked off and letting everyone within hearing distance know it.

All of the above applied to Charlotte, as well.

Dropping to the floor, Henry puffed his lower lip into a bona fide pout. "This was supposed to be fun. Those babies aren't smiling and this isn't fun, hearing them cry so much. I want to play on the swing set, like Dylan said I could. Or...or...I'll go to the mall if you want!"

"You want to leave the babies here, alone?" Chelsea asked. "That isn't like you, Henry. They need us, and their parents are counting on us to take good care of them."

"I don't wanna leave them alone. I just want them to stop being so loud!"

"We do, too, buddy," Dylan said. "And we're trying."

Jinx made a strange yappy-yippy sort of bark, as if she meant to commiserate with Henry, and nuzzled her nose against the boy's hand. The whippet—basically, a miniature greyhound—loved kids of all ages, though she disliked most full-grown men on sight. It had taken months of visiting before she'd warmed up enough to stop yanking at Dylan's pant legs to tug him toward the front door, and several additional weeks until they'd officially become friends.

"She likes you, Henry." Dylan patted Alexander on his back and kept right on rocking, which solved nothing. His nephew continued to cry. Chelsea wasn't having any better luck with Charlotte. "Jinx has her own set of toys downstairs in the kitchen. Maybe you can bring a couple of them up here and play with her in the hallway? That should be a lot more fun than this."

Henry bolted to a stand. "I'll go get some."

"Come right back," Chelsea called as he raced from the room. Then, to Dylan, she said, "This has to stop soon, right? I mean, how long can two babies cry?"

"I don't know, but…probably for as long as they want."

In that second, as if in joint agreement, both babies increased the volume and the strength of their wails. Dylan stopped rocking and Chelsea stopped pacing.

"We have to try something else," Chelsea said, determination lighting her gaze. "This is obviously not working. And the definition of failure is to keep doing the same thing while expecting a different outcome. So…what else have you got up your sleeve?"

"Ah…I'm open for suggestions," Dylan said, recognizing the semisarcastic tone coating his words. "Sorry. Guess I'm frustrated, too. This isn't Alex's usual behavior, and even when Charlotte gets going, it's not normally for this long. I honestly don't know what to try next."

"But you've known them their whole lives! And you like to fix problems, so—"

"Yup, I do, but who doesn't? And yup, I have. But you've actually had a baby. I haven't." More sarcasm. It seemed Henry wasn't the only person on the verge of a temper tantrum. "Sorry, again. But this is the first time I've taken care of them without Reid or Daisy being here, and as I said, this isn't the twins' typical behavior." Rising to his feet, trying to conceive of a solution, he said, "Why don't we try switching what we're doing? Maybe walking will calm Alex and rocking will soothe Charlotte?"

"Doesn't hurt to try, but I have a feeling—"

"I'm back and I brought a squeaky hot-dog toy and a ball that jingles." Henry squeaked the plastic toy and shook the ball. The dog's ears perked at both playtime noises and dashed to Henry's legs, whining and leaping toward his hands. Smiling now, Henry waved the toys near the dog and said, "You wanna play with these?"

"Looks like she does," Dylan said. "Why don't you save your ears and take her into the hallway? Maybe if she's not making so much noise in here, the babies will quiet down, too."

Nodding, Henry left the room and Jinx followed. Whew. Two fewer unhappy souls to worry about at the moment. "Hopefully, that will keep them occupied for more than a minute," Dylan said, walking to where Chelsea stood. As soon as he was within spitting distance, Alex bobbed his fuzzy head toward Chelsea, and lo and behold, his cries slowed down. "Well, look at that. Seems he's smart enough to want the pretty lady in the room instead of the grouchy uncle."

"Um. I don't think so." Chelsea brought Charlotte closer to Alex so she could see her brother, and bam, her cries slowed, as well. "My goodness. They want each other, Dylan."

"Seems that way, doesn't it?"

In silent accordance, they put the babies in one of the cribs so they were lying next to each other, and stood and watched and waited. Within the first minute, their cries completely disappeared, replaced by gaspy breaths of air as they calmed themselves down. Whether it was instinctive or purposeful, Dylan didn't know, but within the next minute, their hands were touching and within two more, both babies were at peace and sleeping.

Wasn't that something?

"I've heard twins have a special bond," Chelsea said, her voice barely above a whisper. "Based on this, I'd say we've just proven that's true."

"They're remarkable, aren't they? Now that they're not screaming."

"Oh, they were remarkable when they were. We just didn't know what to do for them. Those poor babies, being saddled with us as caregivers." A soft, quiet laugh escaped, and she angled her body toward his, her eyes sparkly and her hair loose around her face, somewhat of a mess, and again, he couldn't say if it was instinct or if he'd just been waiting for the proper moment, but he couldn't resist. Didn't want to, either.

"Come here," he said, his voice gruff and full of need. "Please?"

Whether it was the *please* or the tone in which he'd spoken, he had zero idea, but she did as he asked and inched herself closer. That delicious, intoxicating scent of hers wove around him, and without wasting another second, he grasped her arms and pulled her to him. He *had* to kiss her. The thought of not doing so was impossible. "If you don't want to be kissed, say so now, because I'm warning you, I'm less than a second from—"

"Do it, then," she said in a sultry-sweet sort of hum that stole whatever common sense of his remained. "Before one of those babies wakes up or Henry waltzes in or your brother and—"

He groaned and brought his mouth down to hers, silencing her instantly. Her lips were soft but demanding, sweet but searching, and the taste of her was enough to bring a man to his knees. And then some. Hell, if he could kiss this woman every day, he'd give her anything she asked. The sun. The stars. That friggin' car with a trunkful of diamonds and gold nuggets.

Anything she wished, he would make it hers. Just for her kisses.

She moaned—a light, airy, barely there type of sound—and his blood grew hotter. His desire became more profound. His need more desperate. Spreading his palms on the small of her back, he pressed her slender body tighter to his and deepened the kiss. All the while wishing they were somewhere else. Somewhere more private. Somewhere they couldn't be interrupted and he could pull her sweater off over her head and feel the heat of her bare skin against his.

"Dylan," she mumbled, breaking their contact. Her hand went to her hip. "I'm vibrating."

Odd way to describe the sensations the kiss had brought forth, and that she'd done so without batting an eyelash made him chuckle. "Vibrating, huh? I'd say that's a good thing."

A fiery blush trickled into her cheeks. She pulled her cell from the pocket of her jeans. "I meant…um…yes, that, too, but I have a phone call." Glancing at the display, her brows rose in confusion. "I should… I need to take this. Can you go see what Henry's up to?"

He nodded and pivoted, curious as to who was on the phone that required privacy but not overly concerned. His thoughts were too focused on that kiss. And what it had done to him.

Just as he stepped into the hallway and was about to close the door, Chelsea said, "Joel? Why are you calling me now, after so inexcusably long, and how did you get this number?"

In a New York minute, every ounce of desire evaporated. Who was Joel, and what had kept him from contacting her for so inexcusably long, and why was he phoning her now? And was that surprised tremble he'd heard in Chelsea's voice the happy, relieved type of shock or did it fall more onto the annoyed, I-don't-ever-want-to-hear-from-you-again side?

Questions he didn't have the answers for. However, he sensed this Joel person was important. Whether of the good or bad variety remained to be seen, but Dylan's brain was already sending him all sorts of danger signals.

Hell. A red flag. Now. Just as he was beginning to relax.

Chapter Ten

Chelsea's first week of employment passed in a smooth and efficient fashion, mostly due to Haley's decision to start off at a slow pace. Meaning, the majority of those initial twenty-some hours of on-the-job training were all about the basics of how the camp operated.

Details such as when the camp was open—every other week from October through December and February though early April, since the camp's program met the state's criteria for alternative learning, and then again in the summer, between mid-June and the end of August—the criteria Gavin and Haley used to select which boys would form each group, and finally, the various activities and skills the boys were introduced to during the three sessions, many of which were based on the season.

And Chelsea was grateful, not only for the intended practical purpose of easing into her new responsibilities, but also for hanging on to her sanity. Too many distractions and concerns were already circling her brain. Kissing Dylan, for one. The phone call from Joel, for another. And yes, her son's ever-growing bond with Dylan.

Rounding out those issues were her still-important goals of proving her worth to Gavin and Haley and, of course, planning for the future. So, yes, she appreciated that Haley hadn't tossed her into the deep end right off the bat.

But now they were midway through week two, and none of Chelsea's distractions or concerns had disappeared. Or even lightened. While she hadn't spent as much time with Dylan the past week and a half as she had the first, he'd still been around fairly often. And no, they hadn't kissed again, but there was this…electricity between them that couldn't be denied.

At least, not by her.

Dylan's warmth and camaraderie toward Henry hadn't changed one iota, which was good. Amazing and wonderful. Toward Chelsea, though, he wasn't as…oh, hell, she didn't know the word. He was still friendly. He still smiled and teased and seemed interested in getting to know her. There was just this edge to his personality she hadn't seen before. As though he was watching and waiting for her to do or say something, or turn into a completely different person, or…again, she couldn't put her finger on what.

It bothered her, though, whatever it was. Even if it shouldn't.

Joel's phone call had come at the worst possible moment, and frankly, she hadn't had her wits about her to have that conversation then. And when Dylan asked who had been on the phone, she'd told him it was a wrong number. She just wasn't prepared to share certain details of her life, and yes, that included the man who'd abandoned her and her son.

The second Joel had mentioned he was calling about Henry, she'd put him off with the promise that she'd get back to him in a few days. As of now, she hadn't had the strength to do so, and she wasn't sure if she should even bother to make the attempt.

For one, Joel's name was not on Henry's birth certificate. Therefore, unless Joel took her to court to change the status quo, and was actually able to do so, he had zero legal rights. And so far as she was concerned, he'd lost his automatic biological rights by vanishing into thin air, without offering any emotional or financial support to his son.

On the other hand, if by some miracle Joel had become a better person and sincerely wanted to be a real father, then wasn't she just hurting Henry by keeping them apart? God. She didn't know. Was afraid to speculate in either direction. And mostly, she just hoped Joel would disappear into the ether for a second time. Unfortunately, she had the nagging, sickening foreboding that he wasn't done with whatever he'd started.

And no, she hadn't heard from Joel again. That could have something to do with her decision to keep her cell off and only turn it on to check messages. So far, no messages from him—either text or voice—though she did have one from Lindsay a few nights ago. *Kirk* had given Joel her phone number, and Lindsay had apologized profusely, but that didn't really help the situation. Worse, the chance now existed that Joel might know where she lived, so—

"You're somewhere else today, aren't you?" Haley asked. They were currently ensconced in a small office on the ground floor of the farmhouse, and Haley had just opened what appeared to be a financial spreadsheet. "Hope it's somewhere beautiful. Like Fiji or the Bahamas."

"Sorry, Haley. I am somewhere else today, but maybe I should refocus my daydreams," Chelsea said lightly. "And pretend I'm on a beach with an umbrella drink."

"So you were daydreaming, huh? Anything to do with my one remaining single brother?"

"Dylan's great for Henry," she said, pointedly ignoring Haley's underlying question. "He has a way with kids and Henry's responded well to his attention. Well, also to Gavin's."

At the moment, Gavin had Henry somewhere on the property, under the guise of requiring help with cleaning up some of the debris—since a lot of the snow had melted—from the campsites they'd be using once summer got under way.

"Gavin enjoys spending time with Henry," Haley said. "He told me last night that Henry was asking him about hot-air balloons and how he knew he wanted to marry me."

Chelsea laughed. "Henry has a…let's call it a thirst for knowledge." Inside, though, she wondered if her son was still thinking about Sophia and the small size of their family. If so, it meant her little boy was wanting more than she had the power to give him. The thought weighed on her, adding to the already potent mix of her jumbled emotions. *Not now.* She was supposed to be working. "Speaking of knowledge, this spreadsheet appears to be a budget for the camp?"

The other woman didn't respond, just watched her with those steady brown-green eyes, as if waiting for Chelsea to say more. When she didn't, Haley sighed and got back to business.

"Not exactly," she said. "Though this information is used for the budget." She ran her finger along the bottom of the screen. "There are four separate sheets in this workbook. Three of them detail the different types of funding we receive, and the fourth is a compilation of the totals from each. At the moment, we receive money from a few state and federal sources, donations from fund-raising and marketing efforts and…well, contributions from my family."

"Okay, I think I'm with you so far."

"Good. What I want to show you is how to handle the money as it comes in, how to identify the source—especially if it's from one of our marketing or fund-raising campaigns, so we know what's working and how well—and how to enter the information on these spreadsheets."

Feeling slightly overwhelmed, Chelsea nodded. "I hope I catch on fast. I'd hate to make a mistake while you guys are gone."

"You won't, because you're going to have plenty of practice, and it isn't like we receive tons of checks every day." Haley opened a fat file folder. "These are copies of checks we've already processed, from…oh, the past six months or so. I thought we'd pretend they're new and I'll show you step by step what needs to be done. Once you have the hang of it, you can go through the rest on your own."

They worked side by side for the next hour before Chelsea felt confident enough to continue without Haley's guidance. None of what she'd learned was overly difficult, but it did require strict attention to detail. Which turned out to be exactly what she needed.

Time zipped by, and before too long, Gavin and Henry had returned. She took a break to get Henry situated with a snack and a television program. He had a new list of questions from his outing with Gavin, which she answered, and after hugs and kisses, she returned to the office.

Gavin was sitting on the edge of Haley's desk, and they appeared to be in deep conversation. Not wanting to intrude, Chelsea started to back out of the room. Gavin motioned her to join them. "Come in, Chelsea. We're just wrapping up the wedding details."

"Wrapping up? I didn't realize you'd started."

"Told you we wanted this simple," Haley said with a wide, happy grin. "Counting my family, Gavin's mom, you and Henry, and a few of our friends, we're talking a total of—if they all show—twenty guests. Small and fun and so, so easy to plan."

"Have you decided how you're going to get everyone here?" Chelsea retook her chair at the desk. She hadn't expected to be invited to the wedding, but she was pleased to hear that she and Henry were included. It made her feel accepted. "And is there anything I can do to help?"

"We were just talking about those very things," Haley said. "Both of them, in fact. As to the first, I think we're just going to send invitations to a barbecue, but with a line of text that says there's a special reason for the gathering. That should bring most of the people we want here."

"Ah...are you guys sure you're set on this surprise wedding theme?" Personally, Chelsea loved the idea, but she knew Dylan still had his doubts. And honestly, if Haley was worried about people attending because they didn't know, then maybe they should reconsider.

"Oh, we're sure," Gavin said. "If we let this slip, the guys will insist on having a bachelor party, and the girls will just have to throw a bridal shower, and there'll be wedding registries to complete and we'll be running around like crazy people when all we need is a party."

"Exactly. And that is where your other question comes into play." Oh, no. Unless Chelsea was mistaken, an entirely devilish gleam had entered Haley's gaze. "I need your help," Haley said. "Well, yours and Dylan's, since you're the only two who know."

"What do you need?"

"Brace yourself, Chelsea," Gavin said. "Because I doubt you'll be expecting this."

"Hush, you."

"Yes, sweetheart." With that, he stood from the desk and walked to the door. "I think I'll just check in on Henry, see how he's doing right about now."

Narrowing her eyes, Chelsea said, "What is it you want me and Dylan to do that you can't do yourself?"

"Get my mother's wedding dress without her knowledge." A flash of humor crossed Haley's face. "I went to her house yesterday, when she and Dad were at the pub, and looked through every one of their closets. The storage space under the stairs, too. Couldn't find it anywhere, and I have no idea where else to look. So, since I can't exactly ask her myself, I need you and Dylan to figure out where the gown is. And get it."

Chelsea blinked. "Oh. Is that all?"

"Yep!" Haley said, her tone overly bright. "Should be a piece of cake, so long as you two can find where she's keeping the darn thing. And Gavin and I will watch Henry whenever you and Dylan decide to give this a shot. Will you try?"

"Um…have you talked with Dylan about this yet?"

"Nope, but he'll do it," Haley said with confidence. "He might balk at first, express again how I should just tell Mom, but he won't say no."

Chelsea bit her lip in thought. Might be fun, going on a mission with Dylan, and she couldn't deny the appeal of spending time alone with him.

"So long as Dylan is willing, I'm in. But if we have to straight out ask your mom where the dress is, I can't conceive of an excuse that will keep your name out of it."

"Thank you! I'm sure you two will be able to come up with a perfectly believable reason." Satisfaction simmered in Haley's voice. "Once you put your heads together, that is."

"We're supposed to do something tomorrow afternoon with Henry," Chelsea murmured. "If you get Dylan's agreement by then, we can probably discuss some ideas while we're out."

"Terrific!" Winding a long chunk of hair around her

finger, she said, "And I have this feeling that you two will make the perfect team. My feelings are rarely ever wrong."

Another imagined double entendre or an actual one? "You are solely referring to the wedding dress heist, correct? Because that sort of sounded as if—"

"Why, what else would I be talking about?" Haley interjected with a sweet, entirely innocent smile. Sweet, yes. Innocent? Chelsea didn't think so. "Oh! Are you and my brother becoming romantically involved? Gavin and I have a bet going on you two, because I've wondered. I'm for it, in case you're curious."

A bet? Lovely. "Sorry, Haley, but Dylan and I aren't romantically involved." Not a fib. One kiss did not a relationship make. "I'd back out of the bet if I were you."

She gave Chelsea a long, uncomfortable and appraising once-over before shaking her head. "Nope, I don't believe I will. As I said, I'm rarely wrong on these types of matters. We'll just see how this turns out, and... I know! You can join the bet, if you want."

The thought was so ludicrous, so entirely inappropriate, Chelsea burst into laughter. Big, breath-stealing gulps of laughter, which then, without any warning and almost instantly, became big, breath-stealing sobs that tore from her chest with such strength, such ferocity, it hurt. Out of nowhere, the stress, pressure, worries and fears from the past few weeks—hell, probably the past few years, and then some—bundled together and...exploded.

And once the tears started, they refused to stop.

"I—I'm sorry," Chelsea said through the gust of overpowering emotion. She sucked in air, tried to calm herself and failed. "I don't kn-know why this is happening right now."

Haley vaulted from her chair and closed the office door, which gave Chelsea more privacy, and then knelt next to her. She rubbed Chelsea's arm and in a soothing voice said, "Because whatever garbage you have bottled up inside has decided it needs to come out. So, let it. There's nothing to be embarrassed over. Nothing to feel bad about. Just let it out."

And so she did. She hadn't cried—*really* cried—in front of another person in years. Not since her grandmother's funeral, when she raged at the bright yellow sun and the robin's-egg-blue sky and the freshly cut green grass and the fragrant blossoming flowers. How could the world smell so pretty, be so lovely and fresh and *normal*, when Chelsea had lost the only person who'd loved her for *her*, just as she was? Unfair, yes, but also terribly and undeniably cruel.

Since then, she'd kept the worst, the most painful of her tears private.

But today, she cried. Hard and heavy, gut-wrenching tears, and she did so for a long, long while. Haley stayed right beside her. She seemed to know that talking—even the consoling and kind words she could, probably would, say—would increase Chelsea's discomfort. And strangely, somewhere in the middle of the outburst, Chelsea began to welcome Haley's silent vigil, rather than feel embarrassed. She began to find solace in the other woman's company.

Finally, thank God, the tears came to a sniffling, choking, gasping end. Haley brought her a glass of water and again waited quietly. Patiently.

When Chelsea found her voice, she said, "Thank you."

"You're welcome. That's what friends are for."

And that was it. She didn't ask any prying questions, and better yet, she didn't act as if she expected an explanation. But she had declared herself a friend to Chelsea.

A friend. How about that?

"I'll get your wedding dress, Haley," she said. "With

or without Dylan, and I don't know how, but I will. Because…that's what friends are for."

"Push me faster, Dylan!" Henry screeched from his perch on a swing at one of the larger local play parks. Grinning, Dylan did as he was told and added a bit more muscle when the swing came back his way. "And higher. Faster and higher and faster and higher!"

It was one of those wonderfully cool-edging-into-warm spring afternoons. Still too chilly for short sleeves, but warm enough to go without a jacket during the daylight hours. And while Dylan enjoyed skiing and snowboarding in the winter, as well as hiking and camping in the summer, he loved this in-between type of weather the most.

With his wonky work schedule as of late—helping with inventory and such at the sporting-goods store most weekday mornings and his normal shift at the pub most evenings—hanging out at the park on a day such as this was the perfect break. To refuel. To relax.

And yes, though it nearly killed him to admit it, to be with Chelsea and Henry.

They were in his thoughts on a consistent basis now, even when they weren't together. There he'd be, minding his own business and doing his own thing, and bam, there they were, taking up brain space. Of course, Henry was a great kid. Perhaps the greatest kid Dylan had ever met. And naturally, kissing Chelsea hadn't helped him *not* think of her. Just the opposite.

He gave the swing another solid push, his thoughts retracing the day at Reid and Daisy's. Dylan had been relieved to learn some of the specifics regarding the job Chelsea had lost upon arriving in Steamboat Springs. He'd also been annoyed that she'd given the information when Reid had asked, but hadn't with him.

Still. That kiss. One kiss, just one, and the taste of her

had rooted itself in his memory. Truth was, even with all the unknowns, if not for that damn phone call and the small bit he'd caught of that conversation, he'd be flying pretty high.

When he'd asked Chelsea about the call, she'd passed the whole thing off as a wrong number. Which he flat-out knew wasn't true. And *she* should know he knew it wasn't true, since she'd asked for privacy. For some reason, though, he hadn't yet told her what he'd heard. For now, he was caught in the uncomfortable holding pattern of waiting and hoping.

Waiting for her to say something on her own, without him pressing her for information. Hoping he had nothing to worry about. Waiting for another red flag to appear. Hoping there wouldn't be one. Mostly, though, he kept hoping his heart was correct and his brain was wrong.

Chelsea's bubbly laughter drew Dylan's attention to the present. And he had to smile again. She stood in front of Henry, smartly far enough back not to be horse kicked by a pair of little-boy feet going at warp speed, wearing a pair of faded powder-blue jeans and a long-sleeved pale pink shirt. She'd worn her hair loose, so it waved gently around her face, and her lips and cheeks were a delicious rosy shade.

She looked, dammit, as adorable as ever.

"Sweetie, you're going so fast, all I see is a blurry red form," Chelsea called out, referring to the boy's bright red sweatshirt. "You are holding on tight enough, aren't you?"

"Mothers can be such worrywarts," Dylan teased, using a voice just loud enough to carry to Chelsea. She wrinkled her nose at his words and then stuck out her tongue. Yup. Adorable. And he wished she was a little less so. "Isn't that right, Henry?"

"She just don't want me to fall," Henry yelled, the wind-tunnel created by the swing sucking away a good bit of his volume. "I'm A-okay, Mommy! And I don't have to hold on real tight to not fall. I can clap my hands and everything! Watch this, you'll see—"

And then, of course, he flew off the swing like a rocket ship launching into space. Or, in Henry's case, he didn't go up, up, up and away, but rather he sort of went up, then out, then out some more and then…down. Hard. If not for Dylan's instant panic over Henry's well-being, he would've been rather impressed at the distance the kid covered before hitting the ground.

"Henry!" Chelsea got to him before Dylan did, seeing how he'd dropped pretty much directly in front of her. He'd fallen *almost* face-first, but had pulled himself into a leaning-back sitting position using his hands as support. And oh, jeez, he looked more scared than Dylan had ever seen a kid look. And *that* scared Dylan.

One huge helping of undiluted fear coming right up.

"He's breathing," Dylan said, as much to appease himself as Chelsea.

"Talk to me, sweetie," Chelsea said, her voice strong. Capable. "What hurts?"

But Henry just sat there with that fearful expression and didn't try to talk. He wasn't even crying. In shock, Dylan guessed. Lowering himself next to Henry, he ran his hands over the boy's legs and then his arms. "Seems okay so far," he said to Chelsea. Then, "Henry? How about trying to move your legs for me? But stop if it hurts too much. Think you can do that?"

Henry blinked once. Twice. And then nodded. He bent one leg at the knee and then the other, wincing slightly, but that was to be expected. Okay. Good so far.

"Excellent," Dylan said. "Now, let's try the same exact thing with your arms." Again, Henry was able to move and bend his arms. He even raised them above his head. "Whew, good job. I think you're okay." Dylan closed his eyes and sent a brief prayer of thanks upward. To Chelsea, he said, "How about you, honey? You're paler than the flying whiz kid here."

The term of endearment fell from his tongue before he could yank it back in. That, even with his concern over Henry and Chelsea, annoyed him. He wasn't prepared, couldn't get there as things now stood, to declare her his honey or his sweetheart or any other lovey-dovey nickname. Thankfully, she didn't seem to notice his slip.

"I'm fine, just shaken," she said, her voice now wobbly and uncertain. "Jeez, Henry, you about gave me a heart attack. And…and you're probably going to be covered in bruises by the end of the day. Come here, please—" she opened her arms wide "—I need to hug you for…oh, the next week, at least. Maybe two."

Henry crawled into his mother's lap, and she pulled him in tight, hanging on for dear life. He buried his face in her chest and that was when he finally cried. Gently, though. Quietly. They sat that way for a while—a lot less than a week, but longer than a few minutes—before the kid pushed back and looked at Dylan.

"I have a question to ask you, Dylan." His blue eyes—so much like Chelsea's—were wet with tears. His chin trembled, and when he spoke again, his voice shook, as well. "There's something I want to know really bad, and Mommy says to always ask, 'cause it's better to ask than getting all worried and sad. So if I ask, do you promise and cross your heart that you will tell me nothin' but the truth?"

"I will always, no matter what the question is, be honest with you, Henry. We're friends, and friends don't lie to each other," Dylan said, looking the boy straight in the eyes. He couldn't guess at what Henry might want to know, but based on the child's expression, whatever it was meant a helluva lot. "And you never, ever have to be afraid to ask me anything. Okay?"

Dylan glanced at Chelsea, but she was staring at her son, her confusion clearly evident by her slack jaw and pinched brows. So she didn't know what this was about, either. Interesting.

"Okay, I…" Henry sat up straighter and wistful yearning stole over his features. "I want to ask… I want to know if you're my real daddy and that's why we came here for our fr-fresh start, so you could meet me and I could meet you and we could all be together."

Dylan had to fight hard, harder than he ever had before, to keep his emotions from choking him senseless. Henry had never even met his father?

"Henry," Chelsea whispered. "Oh, honey, I never guessed you would—"

"Chelsea," Dylan interrupted, keeping his tone easy and calm, "Henry asked me this question, and I'd like to answer it. If that's all right with you." Tears, unbidden, weighed behind Dylan's eyes, and these he couldn't halt. Didn't even bother trying.

"If you're sure," she said softly, granting him permission. "Just be careful. Please."

Kind. She meant to say *Just be kind,* and of course he'd be kind. This boy wanted a father. And he wanted *Dylan* in that role. Was there ever, could there ever, be a greater honor?

"I'm so sorry, Henry," he said as a big, fat, unmanly glob of a tear slid down the side of his face, "but no. I'm not your daddy. I'm your friend—your *very good* friend— and proud of it, too. I don't see that changing, so you're stuck with me, anyway. Hope that's okay with you."

Nodding, Henry dropped his gaze to the ground, in a gesture reminiscent of his mother, and said, "Thank you for telling me. I wish…I really wish you were my daddy, but now I know."

What Dylan didn't say—couldn't *and* wouldn't say, for fear of confusing Henry even more—was that he wished the same.

Chapter Eleven

Sighing, Chelsea looked out the kitchen window to watch as the three Foster brothers and Gavin attempted to teach Henry how to play baseball. In deference to his age, they were using a slightly oversize, lightweight baseball, and Henry's bat was broader, to make it easier for him to hit the ball. And she appreciated the men's efforts. She just couldn't tell if Henry was having fun. Or if something as simple as a baseball game could make a difference.

In the days following what Chelsea now referred to as the Park Incident, Henry had become a quiet-as-a-mouse, keeps-his-thoughts-to-himself little boy who seemed to carry the weight of the world on his shoulders. He was sad. He was disappointed. And, she thought, he might even have some anger mixed in with that concoction, as well.

One by one, the Fosters crawled out of the woodwork to band together in hopes of cheering up a little boy. Margaret had baked cookies with him, and then she and Paul had taken him bowling. Cole and Rachel—who was just as nice, just as kind, as the rest of the Fosters—had sprung for a movie night. And Reid and Daisy had brought Jinx over to play.

There had been tickling sessions, more ice flying, board-game playing and last night, Dylan and Henry had built a fort in the middle of the living room and Chelsea and Henry had slept there. Her son had his moments of joy. A smile here, a laugh there, the rare squeal of pleasure or surprise, but they didn't last for more than that moment.

It was disheartening, really. Henry had always had a positive, happy-to-be-me outlook, and she wondered, in the deepest part of her soul, if he'd ever get that back.

"He looks like he's having fun," Haley said, standing next to her. Chelsea hadn't even heard her walk into the room. "And the guys definitely are. They've taken him in, you know. He's one of us now, and that means you are, too."

Such a sweet sentiment for Haley to voice, and a nice one for Chelsea to hear, but the words barely registered. Mostly because, when all was said and done, she wasn't one of them. Henry wasn't, either. Better to be realistic than live in a fantasy world.

Still, she knew her manners, so she said, "Thank you."

"Welcome," Haley said. "Look at him out there. He *is* having fun."

"Right now, maybe, but I'm concerned he won't really bounce back from such a huge disappointment." And if he didn't, that was Chelsea's fault. She'd seen this coming, though not quite in this manner. She couldn't have guessed how Henry had pieced together the move to Steamboat Springs and Dylan's coincidental entrance into their lives. But she'd recognized the bond, and she'd worried about the potential fallout. Turning toward Haley, she voiced her innermost fears. "I'm afraid this has broken him."

"Oh, I don't think that's something you have to worry

about. I mean, I get it. Totally. But he's a resilient kid, and he's young, and over time, this will fade."

No. Haley didn't get it. She couldn't, really, and Chelsea didn't blame her for that failure. She envied her, though. Haley had grown up in a secure, loving, supportive family who accepted her for the person she was. So no, Haley would never understand. But Chelsea did.

While she didn't have precisely the same experience as Henry, she knew the loss he was feeling. Because she'd been there. For her, she'd yearned for what she didn't have—a family like Haley's—and she'd hoped to somehow gain that by becoming the daughter her parents seemed to want. When she'd realized that was impossible, she lost hope. But the yearning?

That did not go away. Ever.

So for Henry the same points held true, except his yearning was for a father. And this yearning had led to the hope that Dylan was his daddy. Now her son was facing the realization that what he yearned for, hoped for, was an impossibility. Because the facts were plain: Dylan wasn't Henry's father, and there wasn't a damn thing she could do about that.

Rather than try to explain any of this to Haley, she formed her lips into a smile. "You're probably right, Haley. Thanks for listening." Then, with a head jerk toward the window, desperate to talk about something—anything—else, she said, "And Dylan and I have a wedding dress to locate. I suppose we could do that today, if you're sure about caring for Henry?"

"Right, the wedding dress. Actually, there's been a development." Haley rolled her bottom lip into her mouth, looked through the window and then back at Chelsea. "Dylan mentioned that he…ah…knows where the dress is, so now it's just a matter of actually, um, getting it. And he can probably do that on his own, but I'd—"

"Oh, that is good news, because I'd feel better staying close to Henry," Chelsea said, relieved. She absolutely would have lived up to her word if Haley still required her help. This made it simpler and guilt-free, on both ends of the equation. "I'm so glad for you."

"Yes, me, too, I'm just a little worried that... Well, never mind. That's not your concern at all, and of course, it's more important that you're with Henry."

"What are you concerned about?"

"Well. Dylan is a man, and men can't really comprehend the importance of a bride's wedding gown, you know?" Haley sighed. "I'm worried he won't take care with the dress, and knowing my luck, he'll drop it in a mud puddle or something."

Chelsea chuckled. "I'm sure that won't happen. You're nervous, that's all, which is completely normal. The wedding date isn't that far off."

"A little less than two weeks from now, which is stunning." Haley bent her head, released a breath. "I keep forgetting it's so close. I keep forgetting that soon I'll be Gavin's wife. I don't know if Dylan's said much, but there was a time that Gavin kept pushing me away. He was resolute in not letting anyone get too close." She raised her gaze to Chelsea's. "Due to his past."

"His past?"

"You know he was mostly raised in the foster-care system," Haley said, her voice quiet and solemn. Sad. "His dad died when he was young—just about Henry's age now, actually—and his mother had her own issues. They're closer now, but when he was a child...she let him down. Repeatedly. When I came along, it took a lot to break through the brick wall he'd built around his heart. So he could see all the good possibilities instead of the worst-case scenarios."

Chelsea swung her gaze to the tall, lumberjack man

who was now playing with her son. The same man with the big, rumbling laugh. The same man who showed such easy affection toward Haley, and now toward Henry. And yeah, the same man who had opened this camp for foster boys. She couldn't visualize him as Haley had described. But now that she had more understanding, it all clicked. As a child, *he* had likely fought pain similar to hers.

The same type of pain that her son was struggling with now.

Yet Gavin *had* found happiness. He'd found *family*. That, Chelsea thought, was pretty damn awesome. So much so, she felt a trickle of hope returning. For herself. For Henry.

Facing Haley again, she grinned, and this time she wasn't faking her cheer. "Then it's doubly—no, *triply*— important that your wedding goes exactly as you guys want. So, if it will make you feel better, I'll go along with Dylan to retrieve your dress."

"Gosh, Chelsea, that's…terrific. Just terrific." Haley clapped her hands, much like a child. "Yes, that is a huge relief. Just huge! Thank you, thank you, thank you!"

Perhaps a little overkill on the excitement level for what should be a simple task, but Chelsea put that down to being a happy bride. And now that she understood more about the couple's journey, she truly wanted their wedding to be perfect. It seemed incredibly important.

As if by viewing *their* happily-ever-after, she might be able to locate one for herself. *And* for Henry. To start, she had to work harder at trusting in the goodness she saw around her.

In the goodness she saw in Dylan.

What in the blazes was his sister up to? Frowning, Dylan focused on the road—not that he had any idea where to go—and put the facts together as he knew them.

Haley and Chelsea had strolled into the backyard, arms crooked together, and had called him over. His sister had winked. In triplicate, even. And had stated it was time to hijack their mother's wedding gown, and Chelsea was ready to do so right that very minute.

When he asked Haley if she'd lost her mind, she'd interrupted him with a whispered—so Reid and Cole wouldn't hear, he assumed—tirade on how what a bride wore on her wedding day was immeasurably important, and that she *needed* her brother to do this one thing for her, and if he objected, she would likely burst into tears. Chelsea had then cast a stony glare upon him and said that they *were* doing this, and they were doing it *now*, so he shouldn't bother arguing.

And then, while Dylan was still trying to mull that over, Haley had pushed herself into his arms for a hug and whispered, "Go along with this, big brother. You can thank me later."

So he did just that, but damn if he could figure out why.

There was no wedding dress to hijack, as Dylan had retrieved the darn thing close to a week ago. It hadn't even been difficult to get. You just had to know where to look.

Shortly after Christmas, one of his mother's friends had found *her* dress a moth-eaten disaster, which had sent her daughter into a spin, as she'd planned on wearing it. Margaret Foster, with hopes that Haley might want to wear her dress when she married Gavin, then went out and bought a special preservation box for storage. To keep it safe from the ravenous moths.

The only reason Dylan knew any of this was because his father had complained that the box took up too much room in the closet, so in a fit of frustration one morning, he'd shoved it under their bed. A quick trip to his folks' house when they weren't home and problem solved.

Haley was aware of the entire friggin' story, because

he'd told it to her when he put the dress in her grateful arms, on the very same day he'd grabbed it.

And now, while he wasn't against having Chelsea to himself for a few hours, he didn't quite know what to do with her, because he figured the second she learned there wasn't a wedding dress to hijack, she'd want to turn around and go home to Henry. He understood this, felt much the same way himself, but also thought he should take advantage of this opportunity.

Perhaps they could go to his place. Make some food together, talk, and he could try to make her laugh. He'd been almost as worried about her as he had Henry. Maybe he could get inside her head a little more, find out what the deal was with Henry's dad, whom he was beginning to think was this mysterious Joel, and—

"You're going in circles," Chelsea pointed out, her voice holding a good deal of humor. And yeah, he was going in circles. Just not in the way she meant. "We've driven down this road a total of three times, and I doubt you're lost. What's up?"

"Trying to decide a few things, and I got lost in my thoughts," he said, going left at the light instead of the right he'd already taken three times in a row. "But I'm on course now."

They'd go to his house. Once they were inside, he'd tell her the truth about the dress and try to convince her to stay for a few hours. Beyond that, his ideas were all over the place. And until they were in that moment, he didn't know if he'd listen to what his heart wanted him to do—which pretty much boiled down to another kiss, and then another, and then whatever else might follow—or if he'd hush that side of him in favor of gaining information.

The problem was that he wanted both. In equal measures. And he was beyond sick and tired of holding back, of pretending that he wasn't already three-quarters of the way gone for this woman and her child. Wouldn't take much to push him that last 25 percent, either. Not much at all. If Chelsea saw, felt, even a glimmer of what he did, they could stop wasting time and start being together now. As in, *right* now.

Today and tomorrow, and—if his instincts were true and right—many more tomorrows after that. A lifetime of… Whoa. He was getting carried away. By a helluva lot.

Dylan's heart pumped a fraction harder, a percentage faster. Forget the big unknowns for the moment—what about the small ones? He didn't know her favorite…anything. He didn't know if she was a night owl or an early bird. He didn't know if she preferred beer over wine. He didn't know if she soaked in a tub or took quick, brisk showers.

Or…yuck…did she eat anchovies on her pizza?

Nope, he didn't know any of the answers to those questions, but he thought he might just know *her* well enough to be able to guess. Risking a glance toward Chelsea, he caught her smiling at him and his pulse sped up another fraction.

"Got a few questions for you," he said. "And I'd appreciate some honest answers."

"Now you sound a lot like Henry did at the park," Chelsea said, her voice weighted with the memory. "But sure, I'll either answer honestly or tell you I'm not answering at all."

"Good enough. First up…before you had Henry, were you a night owl or an early bird?" His guess: night owl all the way.

Out of the corner of his eye, he saw her lips quirk. "Night owl. Next?"

"You walk in a bar and order…what?" He figured beer. Probably a microbrew.

"Depends on what I'm thirsty for, but—again, before

Henry—my drink of choice was usually plain old beer. From the tap, whatever was cheap enough for my budget."

He winced at the cheap comment, knowing a lot of what she drank in those days he likely wouldn't consider drinkable. Still, he added a point in the win column. "Okay, this question assumes you're not in any sort of a hurry." He turned into the driveway of his house, a small two-bedroom ranch on the edge of the city. "Do you prefer showers or long soaks in the tub?" *Showers*, he thought, though he couldn't say why.

"Um…showers. Why all these questions? And whose house is this?"

"Wait a minute, I'm not done. There's one more left to answer, and this one," he said, shutting off the ignition, "is the most important of them all. You're ordering pizza—just for yourself, mind you, so no sharing with anyone—what toppings do you get?"

"Everything under the sun," she said with a quizzical and too-cute arch of her brows.

"Everything?" Hell. He supposed they could always get two pies. One for him and Henry, one for her. Because no way, no how, would that little boy want to eat tiny fish mixed in with sauce and cheese. "As in, literally every topping the place offers. No deletions?"

"Well, okay, not quite every last thing," she amended. "Almost everything. I would skip the hot peppers and anchovies, but double up on the cheese and mushrooms. Again, why?"

"No real reason, other than curiosity," he said, resisting the urge to pound his chest and scream in victory. "Ready to go in?"

"Um…sure." She tucked a strand of hair behind her ear and glanced at the house. "The dress is inside, I'm guessing, but who lives here?"

"Yes, my mother's dress—soon to be Haley's—is inside, safe and sound from the elements." Technically, he hadn't lied. The dress was inside, safe and sound. It just wasn't inside *here*. "And, ah, this is my house. I live here."

Blink. Blink. Blink. "Oh." And one more for good measure. "Sure. I'm confused why…that is… Oh, never mind. Let's go in."

Perhaps he shouldn't feel so inordinately pleased that he'd nailed every single question he'd asked Chelsea, but he did. Made him think that, perhaps, his instincts weren't leading him straight into another catastrophic mistake. Made him think he *should* let his heart call the shots.

Maybe he'd swallow his pride, his fears, his *logic*, and tell Chelsea that he thought they could be something together, and that he'd like to walk—not jog or run or, hell, even move at a fast clip—along that path for a while, to see where it led.

He could do that. Or he thought he could. Wasn't all that much of a risk, was it?

Warm midafternoon sun beat down on Chelsea's shoulders while she waited for Dylan to unlock the front door. In the very few steps to get from the car to the framed entry, she'd come to the conclusion that Haley's dress was not in Dylan's house. She didn't know where it was or why Dylan had brought her here, but she was intrigued enough to go along for the ride.

Well, she also wasn't about to turn down the opportunity of seeing Dylan's home.

From the outside, the chestnut-brown-sided ranch-style house appeared to be small, and the landscaping consisted of a neat row of leafy red bushes on either side of the front door, along with a handful of trees of varying sizes in the yard.

Nothing that would require too much upkeep on Dylan's part. Attractive enough, in a clean, no-muss, no-fuss sort of way. Which, honestly, didn't surprise Chelsea. That was how Dylan was as a man: clean, no-muss, no fuss. She mentally added in sexy, funny and…well, sweet. Because how he'd handled Henry at the park and since couldn't be described any other way.

"Now, I hadn't expected visitors," Dylan said, pushing open the door. "So, um…excuse the minor mess. It isn't bad, but if I'd known you were coming, I would've cleaned some."

He stepped inside and, like a gentleman from a long-ago age, bowed at the waist and gestured for her to enter. Which she did, directly into the living room. Again, she wasn't surprised at what she saw, as the furnishings suited the man.

The sofa and chairs were dark brown leather. Several large throw pillows—burnt orange and toffee in shade— were on the couch, along with a thick, soft-looking forest-green blanket left loose on the cushions, as if Dylan had recently napped there. He didn't have a coffee table, but the end tables were wood, wide and blocky, in a darker shade than the furniture. A matching set of oversize green glass-bottomed lamps perched on each.

He had a few magazines strewn about, all of the outdoor lifestyle variety, from what she could see, and the walls were painted the basic off-white. His decorations were sparse. A lone wooden sculpture of a giraffe and a bowl of potpourri, likely a gift from his mother, sister or a past girlfriend—shudder the thought—and that was it. Nothing hung on the walls, either.

"Don't say it," Dylan said with a shrug. "The place needs a woman's touch. I hear it all the time, whenever my mother or any of the other females in my family stop by."

"I wasn't going to say that." Actually, she despised the idea of another woman putting her mark in Dylan's territory. Even if that other woman was family. "I think, if you chose, some more decorative accents would be nice. But I like it how it is. Uncluttered, right?"

"Wow. You might be the first woman to have ever walked in here and not tried to convince me to buy this or that, or hang this or that, or…" Again, he shrugged, but his eyes were warm and soft and—there was that word again—sexy. "There isn't much, but let me show you the rest, and then we'll…um…deal with the wedding dress."

He was right. There wasn't a whole lot more to see. Straight across from the front door, on the other side of the living room, was the kitchen and dining area. Behind the kitchen, a narrow hallway led to the half bath, laundry room and door to the garage. On the right side of the living room, an angled hallway gave access to the full bathroom, master bedroom and fairly large second bedroom. And that was…it. Perfect for a single person or even a small family.

Like a couple with one child. A son, perhaps.

"I don't know what you were worried about," she said, dislodging the out-of-left-field thought. Obviously, a couple with a daughter could live here, too. "I wouldn't call a few items lying about messy." They returned to the living room. "I'd call this the lived-in look. Your house is nice, Dylan. I like it here."

Red streaks crawled up his neck. Had she embarrassed him? "That's nice of you to say, and I like—" he cleared his throat, tossed the blanket on the sofa to the side, sat down and motioned for her to do the same "—having you here. Should've done it before now. I just didn't think of it until now."

Long-ingrained habit of keeping her distance almost had her choosing one of the chairs instead of sitting so near Dylan on the couch, but she stopped herself midstride, pivoted and sat next to him. And she breathed. Why was she so freaking nervous?

"I've already guessed the wedding dress isn't here," she said, wanting to get to the bottom of that mystery first. "Where is it, though?"

"Haley's house," he admitted, looking a little sheepish. "She's had it for days, so I had no clue what she was going on about when you two came outside and…well, that's why I drove down that street three times in a row. I hadn't quite decided what to do with you."

Do with her? And he'd brought her to his house? Instantly and without provocation, the image she'd had at the ice rink flooded her mind. Him. No shirt. Her. Kissing and touching and… *Stop*. Just. Stop. Flustered, she tried to pick up the conversation. "Why would Haley… Oh. I know why." The bet with Gavin. She was probably hoping to stack the odds in her favor. "I think your sister is playing matchmaker, Dylan. Or trying, anyway."

Casually, Dylan's arm went around her shoulders. "Does she need to try? Haven't we been headed in that direction without any interference from my sister?"

"Um. I…I don't know. Have we?"

"I think we have. In fact, I think it started that first night, when you walked into the restaurant," he said, his fingers barely touching her collarbone. And she shivered. With need. With hope. With…desire. From a barely there touch. "For me, anyhow."

A rush of sensations overtook her. Her heart seemed to do a series of somersaults, her stomach grew warm and whooshy—as if shaken and stirred and then shaken again—and tingles of pleasure sped along her skin. "Really? That very first night?"

"Yes. Really. And I—" He broke off. "Don't go all crazy, okay?"

Her breath hitched in her throat. "Why would I go all crazy?"

Gently, as if she were made of porcelain instead of

sturdy bone, he tipped her head toward him, so she had no choice but to look him in those devastatingly gorgeous eyes of his. Oh, my. They were greener than she'd yet seen. Dark, though. Mysterious, somehow, and riveting. Truly, she could stare into Dylan's eyes for hours. Days, maybe.

"There are some words I want to say to you," he said, speaking slowly. Methodically. "And they're pretty big words. And I want to get them right, but see, I'm afraid they'll twist in my mouth and come out all wrong. So, will you bear with me while I stumble through this?"

She opened her mouth, tried to talk, but her vocal cords seemed out of commission. Rather than squeak, she simply nodded. And smiled.

"I…that is, I've had this battle of sorts going on, and I keep attempting to decide which way to go. And—" He stopped, shook his head. "I'm just going to say it straight out, and you say whatever you want. However you feel about it. Okay?"

She nodded again, still afraid to try to talk.

"I like you, Chelsea. More than is logical in such a short time frame, and I've fought with that, because I was once—" Again, he stopped. Again, he shook his head. "Well, I don't want to get into that just yet. Later, perhaps. If we were to…move into another stage."

Was he saying what she thought—hoped—he was? Probably not. But she had to know, and darn it, she had to know right now. She reached for, and somewhat miraculously, found her voice. Thankfully, she sounded calm. Not squeaky at all. "Another stage? As in…?"

Dylan swiped his hand over his jaw, and there went that muscle. Twitch. Twitch. Twitch. And she had to force herself not to become mesmerized.

"It's like this, Chelsea," he said, his words coming right on top of one another. "You and Henry are in my heart.

I don't know why or how this happened so fast—hell, I didn't know it *could* happen so fast—or why it feels as if I've known both of you my entire life. When the facts are, I haven't. But I think I'm to the place where I'd like to suggest we move forward, if you feel there's a possibility here, between us. Or if you think there could be one."

She blinked. Tried to breathe. Tried to *believe* that any of this was happening and not a figment of her imagination. She wanted to say, planned to say, that she felt the same. That she'd wondered, from day one, if he was the person—perhaps, the only person—she'd be able to let in.

Really let in.

But then she had the thought—the horrible, no-good thought—that Dylan's outpouring had more to do with Henry and his need for a father, and the bond the two had already created. What if…oh, God…what if this was just another of Dylan's attempts to fix a problem? As in "Oh, this kid needs a dad, and I like this kid, so…I'll step in."

A possible scenario, based on what she knew of him. But her heart screamed she was wrong, that she was jumping to the worst-case scenario and that her fears weren't allowing her to see the truth. Another possible—hell, likely—scenario. And in that case, then yes, she'd like to try. She really, really would.

Before she could take such a gigantic step, she first needed to know what he had in mind. "And you're suggesting what, exactly? Move forward how?"

Dammit. She hadn't meant to sound so blunt, for her voice to sound so emotionless. But the question was out there now, so she pressed her lips together and waited.

Dylan's eyes became hooded, impossible to read, and his body tensed. He took a minute, maybe two, to respond, and when he did, it was in a composed, almost-but-not-quite flat tenor. "Well, now, that's a question I've thought a lot about," he said. "I think the best way to move forward is to begin the dating process. If that goes well, then after a while, we can discuss the next step. Rationally. Reasonably."

Rationally, huh? Reasonably, too? "And if it doesn't go well?"

He shrugged. "If it doesn't, no harm. No foul, either."

For him, maybe, but for her? For Henry? She was *this* close to refusing his oh-so-logical offer when he suddenly leaned over and trailed his finger down her cheek. When he cupped her jaw with his hand and tilted her face upward, toward him.

"I didn't say that well," he said, his gaze no longer hooded. And there, she saw…hope and desire and longing. For her. Those last two, without a doubt, were for *her*. "Don't say no."

Electricity all but zoomed into being inside of her, between them, and the silly, romantic part of her soul begged her to give in. To try. Just to see what possibilities might exist.

"Okay," she whispered. "Let's date. Logically and reasonably and rationally."

"Hmm. Maybe we should allow some room for spontaneity?" Now his gaze was most definitely fixated on her mouth. "Because right now, all I can think of is kissing you."

"Then kiss me," she said. "Please?"

Without further discussion, he complied. Thank God, he complied. Crushing her to him, he brought his lips to hers in a slow, thoughtful, searching kiss, until every thought in her head disappeared and all that remained was the heat in her belly. It stretched and climbed and eased its way through her, bringing about shivers of longing and stark, hungry need.

A growly sort of groan escaped from Dylan's throat as his lips hardened on hers, as he deepened the kiss, as his hands slipped inside her shirt and stroked her fever-ish skin. She had the thought that she just might die, right here and right now, due to this man and the way her body responded to him. To his kiss. To his touch. Never before had she felt such fierce want.

She tugged his shirt up and ran her hands over his mus-cular back, enjoying the heat of his skin. Heat brought there by her. By her kisses, her touches, and it was…a powerful realization. Potent and life affirming and…sexy as hell. And all she wanted was to feel more of his hot skin. She wanted to touch and kiss every inch of his body, and she wanted—no, she *ached* and *hungered*—to feel the full weight of him on top of her. Inside of her.

"I want you," she said, pulling her mouth from his, suc-cumbing to the demands, the needs, of her body. Of her heart and of her soul. "Might not be logical at this point, but those are the facts. I want you—" she gulped for air, for courage "—to take me to your bedroom. And then I want to take off all of your clothes, while you take off mine, and then I have this idea—"

That was all she was able to say before his mouth re-claimed hers, before his strong, capable, all-male and *sexy* arms lifted her and he carried her to the bedroom.

As it turned out, he had a few delightful ideas of his own.

Chapter Twelve

Daylight was just creeping into twilight when Chelsea rolled over and found Dylan watching her, his gaze steady and sure, warm and satisfied. She reached toward him, skimmed her hand down that amazing chest of his and smiled, feeling very much like a cat who'd all but guzzled a gallon of rich, heavy cream. Lazy. Happy. And yes, satisfied beyond measure.

Regrettably, real life beckoned.

"I hate to say this," she said, "but I should probably get home soon."

"I know," he said. "First, though, I want to talk to you about something."

"Oh." She pulled herself to a sitting position while keeping the blankets wrapped around her naked body. This couldn't be the morning-after see-you-around speech, because…well, for one, it wasn't the morning after. And, more important, Dylan wasn't like that. Still, she had enough insecurity to ask, "Are you regretting what happened between us?"

"Sex?" His lips curved into a relaxed, teasing smile. "You can say the word, you know."

She wrinkled her nose. "Fine. Are you, Dylan Foster, regretting that we had sex?"

"No, Chelsea Bell, regret is the last thing on my mind right now." He plumped his pillow and turned to his side, all the while keeping his eyes locked onto hers. "But there is something you should know about me, something I should have shared before now."

Apprehension slid in, just a trickle of it, but enough to have her clutching the blankets tighter. She went for the same teasing tone he'd used a minute ago, saying, "Oh. I see. The confession finally comes out. You're the real diamond-and-gold-nugget thief, aren't you?"

"I wish it were that simple, but this is from my past." He closed his eyes for a millisecond, as if searching for the correct words. Then, opening them, he said, "I'm divorced, Chelsea. Have been for years, so this isn't a recent occurrence."

Okay, now this? She hadn't seen this coming, but it didn't threaten her or scare her. People had pasts. They had history. And duh, of course a woman would've snapped up Dylan at some point in time. Heck, she was surprised he was single now.

"I'm not upset that you were once married, if that's what you're worried about."

"Didn't think you would be upset, but I do think if we're going to give this a real shot—in our reasonable, rational and logical way, of course—that you should know about this period of my life. It affected me, Chelsea. Changed me by a huge degree."

Blinking, she nodded. Tried to stay focused on him, on what he needed from her, rather than all the garbage she'd yet to share. Because she knew what he meant. Her past had affected and changed her, also to a huge degree.

Maybe when he was done, if she had the strength, she'd try to tell him about her past, as well. That was a really big *maybe*, though. Huge.

Therefore, in case she couldn't get to where she'd need to be, she gave both of them an out. "If this is important to you, then I'll listen. Of course I will. But, Dylan, you should know that it isn't necessary on my end. I'm fine with leaving the past alone."

His eyes narrowed ever so slightly, but he recovered fast. Nodded. "This feels necessary to me. We just slept together, Chelsea, and I intend to sleep with you again. Keeping these types of secrets from you, the woman who is sharing my bed, seems deceptive. Wrong. And not the best foundation for a successful relationship."

She liked the first part of what he said, the bit about sleeping with her again, and she liked the last part, about their relationship, but she didn't know how she felt about the second. Her life had almost demanded the necessity of keeping secrets. In order to feel safe and sane and… normal. Bringing her knees to her chest, she wrapped her arms around them. "I don't see it in quite the same way, but that doesn't mean I don't respect your side. Because I do."

The air in the room seemed to grow heavier, denser. Lines creased his forehead, and she guessed he was weighing her statement with his own concerns, his own beliefs on what was acceptable and what was not. On what he could live with, if they were to continue.

And dear Lord, did she want to continue.

A long, agonizing minute later, he said, "Well. I suppose that's fair, if not ideal. At least we know where the other stands." And then, while she expected he'd warn her before diving headfirst into his story, he didn't. He just started talking. "I got married young, directly out of high school, to a woman named Elise. I loved her with all the dumb, thick-skulled naïveté only an eighteen-year-old kid can have, and I thought we were meant for each other."

Chelsea's heart thudded, hard, as he spoke, as he talked about Elise and who she was when he met her, the way she'd grown up—eerily similar to Chelsea's upbringing—and then her deceptions. What she'd done to Dylan, to their marriage. The pain she'd brought him.

Oh, he didn't actually say *She stomped on my heart and crushed my soul.* But he didn't have to. She could *hear* his hurt in the staccato, broken beat of his voice. She could *see* the haze of his younger self's pain in the depths of his eyes.

And somewhere along the way, she began to hurt *for* him. She hurt for the man he once was, the man who'd given his love so freely, so hopefully, only to have it tossed in his face. As if the gift of his love meant nothing. As if *he* meant nothing.

When this man? He was so *not* nothing. He was… rather astonishing.

By the time Dylan finished speaking, Chelsea's hurt had morphed into anger. Of the red-hot, blazing sort. And it was a darn good thing this Elise person lived on the other side of the country, because Chelsea wasn't altogether sure if Elise lived here in town that she wouldn't drive there now and…and…tell her how incredibly stupid, how stupendously moronic she was for choosing some other man over Dylan Foster.

Completely. Absolutely. Moronic.

She didn't have the words to express her hurt, her anger. Her rage, really, at what Dylan had gone through. He'd said it had changed him, had stopped him from really living for most of those years in between then and now. And wasn't that a horrible waste?

She sighed, rubbed her hands over her face. Yes. Elise was a moron.

"You're awfully quiet," Dylan said. "What's spinning in that head of yours?"

He asked the question in a careful, cautious, tentative way. Due to this, Chelsea chose to go for humor in the hopes of eliciting a laugh. "Honestly? I have a question. Just one."

"Go for it," he said, still tentative. "I'll… Whatever you want to know."

"Do you have an ax on the premises?"

He gave her a blank look. "What? An ax, you say?"

"Yes. An ax." She mimicked the motion of chopping down a tree. "Do you have one here or do we need to visit the hardware store before we travel to Maine? It's high time that I prove I really am an ace with weaponry. Of all sorts." She offered him her best oh-so-innocent smile and winked. "Axes just happen to be my favorite. So, are you up for a road trip?"

He stared at her, seemingly tongue-tied, for a full ten seconds. She knew this for fact because she counted. Then a roar of laughter burst from his chest. When he stopped, he gave her a broad smile. "You're something, Chelsea Bell. That was not the reaction I was expecting. Here I tell you my deepest, most agonizing secret, and you find a way to make me laugh."

"I hope you don't think I'm making fun of what happened," she said quickly, just to be sure there weren't any misunderstandings. "Or that I don't take this seriously. I do." She blew out a breath and chose to go with the truth. "I'm madder than hell that you went through such a mess due to a careless and heartless woman. It just irks me, badly, because you deserve…"

And there, she halted her speech. How to say what was in her heart?

"I deserve what?" Dylan prodded.

"The best that life has to offer."

"So do you, Chelsea," he said, his voice one notch above a whisper. "So. Do. You."

"Don't say that," she said. "You can't…say that."

"Um. Excuse me? I'm entitled to my opinion, and I already said it, and I still stand by it. You deserve the best that life has to offer, Chelsea."

Sadness, borne of a life that had not delivered her the best—other than her son, the boy who had, in many ways, saved her—had her shaking her head in denial. Tears welled, but she refused to let so much as one of them fall.

She wouldn't taint what had happened here with Dylan by crying.

"Why is it difficult for you to hear that I believe you deserve an amazing, kick-ass life?"

"You can't say that, you can't possibly think that or believe that, not without knowing more about—" *Me*, she thought. *Without knowing more about the pain that lives inside of me. Of where it comes from. Of how it formed me.*

"More about you? Then tell me." Dylan sat up and held her hand in his. "Give me a crash course or a master class on Chelsea Bell. Either one or somewhere in between."

With her jaw clamped shut, she lifted her gaze to stare studiously at the ceiling. This—all of this—was so darn complicated. She didn't talk about her past—not her childhood, not Joel—with anyone. Ever. Doing so, especially with Dylan, would be akin to splitting herself wide-open and saying *Here, take a good, long look and tell me what you think. Do you understand me better now? Do you care? Is it okay that I care so much about you?*

Oh, God. He'd opened himself for her. Could she do the same for him? If a miracle occurred and she could, and he then responded positively, maybe…just maybe she'd be able to breathe—really breathe—around him. Maybe then she'd be able to move on to how much she loved his eyes. His laugh. His capable, strong...*beautiful* hands.

Maybe she'd even be able to tell him how, when they were in the park and Henry had asked his heartbreaking question, she had wished, so very much, that Dylan *was* her little boy's daddy. Because in so many ways he'd already proven that he was worthy of the title.

"Hey, Chelsea?" Dylan rested his head on the headboard, right next to hers, and joined her in her staring campaign. "Feel like telling me what I'm supposed to be looking at?"

Split herself wide-open and let him in...or not?

"Talk to me, honey," he said gently. Persuasively. "I'm not altogether certain of what's going on with you, but I'm right here. I'll listen if you need an ear. Or, if for some reason, you're feeling the womanly need to cry...well, I have a shoulder. Two of them, actually."

Honey. He'd called her honey. And he'd offered her his ear and his shoulder. The yearning to share herself with this man was compelling. Overwhelming. And she came close.

So. Very. Close. But when push came to shove, she couldn't find the will or the strength or the courage. The risk was too darned high.

What if he left her, like her parents had? As Joel had?

She wasn't sure she'd remain standing if that happened, because she thought it was entirely possible that she might just love this man. Might? No, she did. She absolutely did. But that wasn't rational or reasonable, and that was how they'd agreed to move forward. They were just getting started. Dylan had said so himself.

Better to wait, to be sure, before taking a knife to her soul.

She swallowed hard and, forcing a lighthearted laugh, said, "What is it with you and womanly needs? I'm fine,

Dylan. Absolutely fine. Just thinking about the most direct way for us to get to Maine. Flying would be best, but I doubt I could carry an ax onto a plane, huh?"

"They'd probably lock you up," he said, going along with her joke. His voice was strained, though, and…disappointed? Frustrated and sad?

Probably a mix of all three and then some, and she understood. Here, after sharing their bodies in this very bed, he'd shared a piece of his soul. With her. And despite her wishes or her dreams or her hopes, she wasn't a strong enough woman to reciprocate.

"We should go," Dylan said, releasing her hand and reaching over the edge of the bed to grab his shirt. "So you can get home to Henry."

"That would be…good." She started to do the same, reaching for her pile of clothes on the floor, when Dylan's phone trilled. Loudly.

He yanked it from his jeans and answered with a gruff "Hey. What's up? Oh. I don't know, maybe she has it off. She's right here, though. One sec." Dylan half tossed, half slid the cell across the bed toward her. "It's Haley, for you. She tried to get you on your phone, but said the call wasn't going through."

Dang it. A mistake she shouldn't have made, leaving her phone off when she wasn't with Henry. Picking up the cell, she said, "What's going on? Is Henry okay?"

Haley started to talk, in a low, hushed voice, and as each spoken word registered in Chelsea's brain, her world skidded to a halt and then, piece by piece, shredded apart.

Joel was here. At Haley's. And he was waiting for her.

About halfway to Haley's, Dylan couldn't keep his temper to himself any longer. He was mad. Royally so. Only problem was, he didn't know whom the anger was directed at. His brain for being right. His heart for being wrong.

Chelsea for not opening up so they could've avoided the mess they were about to go into, or, hell, so he could have, at the very least, been prepared.

Or was he rip-roaring ticked off at himself? For falling in love with a woman who refused to give him so much as a toehold into *her* heart. Because dammit, that was exactly what had happened. He loved her. He loved her son. The number of minutes, hours, days or weeks they'd known each other no longer mattered one friggin' iota. He loved them.

And that was that.

Could be that he was furious with his sister. She was the one, after all, who'd put the idea in his head that one heart could instantly recognize another. Maybe if she hadn't yapped so much about her immediate bond, her strong connection to Gavin, Dylan would have kept listening to his brain, kept going on with his easy, predictable, comfortable-as-all-get-out life.

Hell. He kind of figured he was furious with the world at large right about now, and everything and everyone in it, but he'd start with Chelsea and this business about Henry's father.

"You told me that Henry's father wasn't in the picture and that Joel's phone call was a wrong number," he said in a growl, stopping at a railroad crossing. Great. Why wouldn't a train be crossing these tracks at the exact moment he was in an all-fired hurry? "Were both lies?"

"You're mad," Chelsea said, her voice quivering with emotion. He almost felt bad, but he reached down deep and kept hold of his temper. "And I get it, but sorry, right now my focus is on Henry and what might be happening. Not on you or your bruised feelings."

"You were right the first time." He was worried about Henry, too. Almost sick with it. Via the quick phone conversation, he knew that Haley had smartly gotten the boy upstairs to his room, while Gavin had sequestered Joel on the back porch. Hopefully, that setup wouldn't have changed any by the time he and Chelsea got there. "I'm mad. Not bruised."

"All right, fine. Let's talk about this," she said tightly. "Yes, I lied about the phone call. I didn't know how to explain it then, and that seemed the easiest route. However, when you asked about Henry's father, Joel was not in the picture. Or he mostly wasn't in the picture. And I certainly couldn't have predicted this, based on his prior behavior."

"And that's what I'm talking about, Chelsea." The damn train was moving at a snail's pace. "I don't know what Joel's prior behavior was. I don't know *anything* about him."

She pressed the palms of her hands to her eyes and he knew, just knew, she was trying real hard to hold it together. Which, yup, made him feel like a total jackass. If he had this ice-cold terror running through his veins over what this Joel person wanted, how must she feel?

Wait. No. *She* knew Joel. She knew what he was capable of, whether good or bad or somewhere in the middle. He knew *nothing*. So Dylan's brain kept circling toward the bad.

Well, hell. Maybe that was the true culprit for the strength of his anger. His boy—*his* boy—could be in danger, and there wasn't a lick of anything he could do about it sitting here at these damn railroad tracks waiting for a sluggish train to *move*.

"Is he dangerous, Chelsea?" Dylan asked, his voice ragged. As soon as the question left his mouth, his temper swirled out the cracked-open window, leaving him with nothing but fear at the horrific possibility. "Is Joel dangerous? Could he potentially hurt Henry?"

"I don't think so," she said softly, tremulously. "I haven't seen him since three weeks after I told him I was pregnant, when he left me for...well, I don't know where he went. He moved away from Pueblo. When we were to-gether, he was selfish and immature and...and careless, but no, he never showed signs of violence."

Dylan didn't like the "selfish, immature and careless" description at all, especially when connected to Chelsea, but the no-violence part was good. It helped, a little, in calming his dread.

"Wait a minute," he said, her words taking hold and digging in deep. "He disappeared when you were preg-nant, and until that phone call, you hadn't heard any-thing from him? Just bam, he left you and his unborn baby alone?"

And just like that, his anger was back, in force.

"He sent me a postcard six—no, seven—months ago. On which he stated he was thinking of me and wanted to say hello. Nothing else before and no, nothing after until he...until he called." A soft, agonized moan slid from her throat. "I told him I'd call back in a few days, but, Dylan, I didn't. I just wanted him to disappear again. So I don't even know why he phoned."

Longest. Slowest. Train. In. The. World.

"Well, I don't blame you for that. This man abandoned you and your child for years. Years, Chelsea. Why would you give him the time of day?"

"For Henry. He deserves a father, a good father. And if Joel... If for some reason, he moved back to Pueblo to try to make amends, to be a real father, then *I've* been selfish."

Selfish? For protecting her son from the idiot who'd walked out on him from before he was even born? No. Dylan didn't agree with Chelsea on that front. Such a man didn't deserve Henry, and Henry deserved a helluva lot better. Still, her explanation had put more of the pieces to-gether, and that helped give him a greater understanding.

"So," he said, "I'm guessing that Joel's return to Pueblo

had something to do with why you moved here, to Steamboat Springs?"

She turned toward him and in a guilt-ridden voice said, "Yes. I…was afraid I'd bump into him somewhere, with Henry, and that Joel would stupidly blurt the truth." She closed her eyes. Sighed. "That would have been a problem, because all I've ever told Henry is that his daddy couldn't stay with us, but that he'd be there if he could. I…planned on telling him more, as he got older. When he could better understand that the failing was Joel's. Not his."

That, too, made sense. The kid was only four.

"Honey," he said, purposely using the term of endearment, "if you'd shared this with me before, I could've helped you figure out what was going on. I could've talked to Joel myself or sat with you while you spoke to him. You do not have to tackle everything alone."

Not anymore, she didn't.

Finally, the train passed and the crossing was clear. Putting the car into gear, he drove over the tracks, slowly upping the car's speed. The faster he got to Henry, the better.

"See, I understand why you would say that, but my life…it's been a lot different than yours, Dylan. I don't know how *not* to go it alone."

Was that a bit of temper he heard in her voice? Why, yes, he believed it was. Deciding to push that button a little, to give her some relief from her worries, he said, "It's easy. You open your mouth and you ask for help. Try it, Chelsea. Say 'I could use some help.'"

"Not that simple," she snapped. "I learned fast that the only person I can count on is myself and, due to Joel and…other significant people in my life, that keeping my distance is the only surefire way to stay safe. So don't go telling me I should have done this or I should have done that. You are not me, and you have no idea what…what…"

And then, dammit, she burst into tears.

"Ah, honey, don't do that," he said. "Please don't do that."

If anything, her tears grew stronger. Louder. And he did not know what to do. He couldn't pull over and hold her right now, not when Henry needed them, and he... Hmm. Perhaps he could do something, after all.

"This is my fault," he said, speaking in a woe-is-me sort of tone. "And I owe you an apology, Chelsea. I've been too nice and kind and helpful. I didn't realize that night I found you in your car that the worst thing I could do was give you a place to sleep. And damn, then I went and offered you a loan. Not once, but twice. Not sure what I was thinking there, so I hope you can forgive me. Good thing the rest of my plan backfired, or I'd have even more to be sorry for."

He heard her suck in a breath. And then another. "What plan?"

"Oh, the one about finding you a job and a place to live, so I could get you and Henry set in your brand-new fresh start. See," he said, turning onto the long, windy road where Haley's house was located, "right from the beginning, all I wanted was to see you smile. And that scared me. A lot. Because of what I told you about Elise."

Her crying became less intense. "I don't understand."

"I fell for Elise fast, Chelsea, and within minutes of knowing you, I was falling harder and faster than I did for her. So yeah, that scared me. Figured the best way to stop that from happening was to get you settled so I wouldn't worry about you and I could keep my distance. But then," he said, "my sister went and offered you a job. And I went a little nuts, trying to decide if you were like Elise or not. If you would...hurt me as she had."

"I...I thought you did set up the job with your sister."

"Nope, wasn't me." Oh, thank God. They were here. He

pulled into Haley's driveway and, once they reached the top, parked to the side of the many cars that were already there. Most of which belonged to his family. Two of them, though, he didn't recognize. "We're here now, honey, so we'll have to put the rest of this conversation on hold."

"Oh!" She unbuckled her seat belt and leaped from the car, started up the path toward the house at a fast clip. He was behind her several paces, and while he wanted to charge in like a gladiator with a sword to protect what was his, he…couldn't. Difficult, that, but she hadn't declared herself to be his, for one thing.

And as much as he hated it, this was Chelsea's battle, and hers alone. Unless she reached for him. Unless she decided to bring him into battle with her.

She stopped. Pivoted and waited for him to reach her. When he did, she licked her lips and twisted her fingers. "I'm scared, Dylan. Real scared," she said. "I don't know what Joel wants, and I…I could use some help. Will you stay with me? See him with me?"

"Of course I will," he said, as if her request fell into the no-big-deal variety of requests. It didn't, though. Not for her, and while he didn't know all of the reasons behind her go-it-alone mentality, he didn't—as he'd pigheadedly thought—require those answers right now. He knew about Joel, and that was a real good start. More than anything, Dylan was just glad she'd reached out to him, so he asked, "Ready to go see what this joker wants?"

Her chin dipped in a slight nod, and they headed toward the house.

Earlier, when she'd refused to share even the tiniest, most minuscule detail of her life—especially after what he'd shared, most especially after she'd trusted him with her body—it had hurt, realizing she couldn't or, he supposed, wouldn't trust him with her secrets. With her heart.

But now, suddenly, Dylan did not care if Chelsea ever

told him her darkest secrets, her deepest pain, so long as she knew she *could*. So long as that decision wasn't made from fear or distrust of *him*, and she understood that he would listen when and if she chose to talk, and that whatever secrets she shared—no matter how dark or how painful—he would guard as his own.

Because Chelsea wasn't anything like Elise.

All of his worries, the comparisons he'd tried to draw between the two women, were his problems. *His* baggage. They weren't Chelsea's. But if his baggage had created such havoc in his thinking toward her, in trusting in and accepting what his heart had declared, then it made perfect sense that *her* baggage could do the same toward him.

His future belonged with Chelsea. With Henry. He might just have to be patient, give her some time to reach the place he had, seeing as how he'd gotten here in the traditional Foster way. Fast and furious with a bit of crazy thrown in. But yeah, he could wait.

And that was, as Henry would say, A-okay.

Chelsea slipped her hand into his and held on tight. He held on tighter. "Thank you," she said. "Because you're right. No one can do everything on their own, and this…I don't think I could have done this alone as well as I will be able to do it with you."

"I'm glad I'm here, honey, more than I can say. But right now, I have a question," he said. "Am I allowed to punch Joel in the jaw?"

"Oh, if he gives you a reason," she said coolly. Matter-of-factly. "Any reason at all, then yes, please do so. Good and hard."

Chapter Thirteen

The second they walked into the house, Margaret appeared from the living room, her smile gentle but her eyes fierce. In a lowered tone, she said, "Henry is upstairs with Haley and Rachel, and—" the older woman reached over and squeezed Chelsea's arm "—don't worry, he isn't aware that anything out of the ordinary is happening."

Chelsea's eyes closed as she sighed in relief. "Thank you, so much," she said. "Please thank Haley and Rachel, too. It's just so nice that you're all here, and…and…"

No. She would *not* cry again. It seemed that once she'd set her tears free in front of Haley, they just wanted to keep on coming. Sensing her discomfort, Dylan rubbed the small of her back, probably to remind her that he was here. With her.

And it was comforting. Strengthening. To know that someone—that Dylan—had her back. Literally and figuratively.

"Oh, sweetheart," Margaret said, "where else would

we be? Daisy would be here, too, if she could. But she had a rough day with the babies, so Reid talked her into staying home."

There were several places that Chelsea figured the rest of the Fosters could be—in their homes, living their own lives—but they'd chosen to be here. And to her, that seemed incredible. Selfless and sweet and…as if the entire Foster family also had her back.

"Is Joel still on the porch?" she asked. As much as she did not want to deal with him, he was here now, so her preference was to get this over with. As fast as possible. So he would leave.

"Hmm. Yes, I believe that is where the men have him penned in." The corners of Margaret's lips twitched. "Why, he had to use the bathroom a little while ago, and Reid and Cole stood sentry outside the door and then escorted him directly back to the porch."

Dylan gave a short nod. "Good. I don't want him anywhere near Henry."

"Neither do any of us." Margaret nodded toward the kitchen. "Go on, do what you need to, and I'll wait here. I'm the designated lookout, in case Henry gets curious."

"Ready, honey?" Dylan asked Chelsea. And okay, she was stunned he'd used the term of endearment in front of his mother. Pleased, though, too. "Or do you need another minute?"

"I could use a hundred more minutes, and then some," she said. "But I'm not sure that would make me any more ready than I am right now. Let's go."

With her hand in his, he led her away from the front hallway and toward the kitchen, where he stopped at the wide-arched entry. Inhaled a sharp-sounding breath, and his entire body went stiff. As if, she thought, he was ready to pounce. She looked at him, at his face, in curiosity and in concern, and saw that muscle in his jaw twitching away.

Noticed his eyes were narrowed, dark and intensely focused on the room they were about to walk into.

Chelsea's heart flutter kicked beneath her breastbone, and she knew—or guessed, was more accurate, since she couldn't actually see past Dylan with the angled, guarded way he stood—that Joel was in there and not on the back porch. She also guessed that Dylan was, at that very second, considering how very much he wanted to punch Joel in the jaw.

So before his temper could win out and he did something that he'd regret later—because if Dylan roared in and hit a man without direct provocation, he *would* feel regret—she pulled herself free from his grip, stepped around him and entered the kitchen.

And blinked. Closed her eyes fully and opened them again. Tried to get her brain to catch up to what was right in front of her. Because unless Joel had grown several inches and added on a solid layer—maybe two—of muscle, the dark-haired man sitting at the table with a perplexed, stunned-appearing Gavin at his side was not Joel Marin.

Dylan, who'd followed her in and was standing next to her, still had that ready-to-pounce, ask-questions-later look, so she rested her hand on his arm. His muscles were tense. Hard. "This isn't Joel," she said quickly. "I don't know who this is, but he isn't Joel."

"Joel's out back. With the men," Gavin said with a nod toward the door. He then glanced at the man next to him. "This here is Logan Daugherty. He's...well—" Gavin ran his hand over his beard. "Turns out he's my half brother, and we've just started talking, trying to unwrap it all. Haley isn't even aware yet, as he only just got here. Seems to be the night for unexpected visitors."

Logan nodded at Chelsea and Dylan, smiled briefly,

but didn't say anything. The poor man was probably wondering what sort of mess he'd walked into.

"Half brother?" Dylan wagged his head back and forth, as if trying to purge an ocean of water from his ears. "I didn't know you had any siblings."

"Yeah, well, that makes two of us. I'm glad to know now, though," he said, directing his statement at Logan. And through the glaze of confusion, Chelsea saw a hint of gladness in Gavin's eyes. He gave a second nod toward the porch. "But you two need to determine what that man out there wants. He's been patient. Friendly enough, in case that matters."

"Patient and friendly don't cut it after close to five years," Dylan said, his tone abrupt. "We appreciate that you kept him away from Henry. And, Logan? Nice to meet you."

Without waiting for a reply, he cupped Chelsea's elbow with his hand and together, they went to the back porch. Joel was sitting on the chair farthest from the door, while Paul and Cole were sitting closest. As for Reid, he stood along the wall, his thumbs in his pockets in a laid-back pose that was anything but relaxed, about three feet from Joel's chair.

The air simmered with an edgy, uncomfortable energy, and despite the many ways that Joel had wronged her and her son—because no, she would not, could not, call Henry *their* son—Chelsea was somewhat impressed that he'd stuck it out and waited.

The second Joel saw her, he started to stand, but Reid turned his head toward him in the slightest of ways, the smallest of motions, and Joel wisely chose to stay put.

He looked the same as she remembered. But since she hadn't seen his face for so long, and in that same chunk of years had watched Henry's features change, she was rather dazed to realize the physical similarities between her son and this man.

The sandy mop of hair she loved to tousle on Henry's head was the same hair on Joel's. Their long, narrow and somewhat pointed jawlines were similar, though Henry's held more fullness. Could be the difference in age, she supposed. And while Henry had her eyes, in color and in shape, the straight slant of his eyebrows came from Joel.

It was odd, but not anything more than that. Just surprising, as when she looked at her son all she ever saw was Henry. She never saw the man who had contributed half of her child's DNA, and she knew the same would continue to hold true, even after whatever happened tonight.

"Want us to leave or stay right here, Chelsea?" Reid asked, his tone calm and clear. There was a warning embedded in his tenor, though. Not for her, she knew. But for Joel. "We are happy to do either, whichever is the most comfortable for you."

"Dylan and I can take it from here," she said. "But I appreciate all you've done, and if you could stay somewhat close, in the event there's an…issue, I would appreciate that, as well."

"I think it's safe to say you can count on that," Paul said, rising from his chair. "We'll be nearby, all of us. That being said, I'd like to believe that Joel is smart enough, compassionate enough, to understand how much better it would be for everyone if an issue did not occur."

Cole stood and approached Chelsea, reached out as if he had the thought to hug her, but pulled back. Still, she noted the gesture and was warmed by it. Then, with a nod of support in Dylan's direction, he retreated to the house. Reid and Paul followed.

Pulling in a breath for strength, she forced her legs to carry her toward Joel, who had yet to speak. She couldn't blame him. The Fosters had, apparently, arrived in record time when they were made aware of Joel's presence and, once here, had put on quite a show. Because they were kind. Because they cared. Because she and Henry were one of them now.

How about that?

All at once, Chelsea knew with absolute, rock-hard certainty that she had nothing to be concerned over. Nothing to fear from Joel. He couldn't hurt her or Henry. Not only would she not allow him to, but Dylan and his family wouldn't, either.

She sat in the chair to Joel's left, while Dylan replaced Reid's efforts at holding up the wall. He angled his arms across his chest in a nonchalant manner, and he cast his gaze toward Joel, his expression flat and unreadable but, as typical, steady.

And then she got to the heart of the matter. "Why are you here?"

"Not to cause trouble," Joel said, the tempo of his speech rushed. "That isn't my goal, but you didn't return my call, and your phone seemed to be off every other time I tried to reach you."

"So you thought you should just come on over, after vanishing from my life for over four years? After proving you have zero interest in *my* son's best interests and welfare?" She crossed her legs and gave that steady gaze of Dylan's a shot. "I think that plan was ill conceived."

"Didn't have much choice," he said. "Time is important here. I'm leaving the country in three days, Chelsea, and I don't know when I'll return." A smile lit his face. "I'm getting married, and my fiancée's accepted a job in Brazil. So…yeah, that's why this had to happen now, if it was going to happen at all. And—"

"Please don't tell me you've had the fatherly urge to meet your son before you take off for greener pastures." Dylan stepped forward and moved to Chelsea's side. "Because if that's what this is about, you can turn around and leave. Henry isn't here to assuage your guilt or your curiosity. So," Dylan said in dark, deep-seated annoyance, "what I need to hear from you is that you're not here to mess up a little boy's life with a clear-your-conscience visit."

"That isn't why I'm here, though I had hoped to... see him, at the very least." A genuine growl came from Dylan's throat, causing Joel to flinch. "Maybe just a picture of him?"

"Why are you here?" Chelsea asked again, her temper rolling into being at the mention, the suggestion, she'd give this man a picture of her son. "If not to barge into Henry's life, then what is it you want, Joel? My courtesy is only going to extend so far. You have no idea—none—of everything I've gone through to keep that little boy safe and happy. And you...you could have helped. You *should* have helped." She blinked rapidly, not because she was near tears, but due to the haze of anger coursing through her blood. "You left us alone."

Dylan's hand came to her shoulder. She reached for it, for him and his strength, and a modicum of peace returned, calming her anger from a flame to a simmering burn. Good thing, too, because she thought she just might have punched Joel in the jaw herself.

"That's why I'm here. To...to apologize for leaving you alone. And this isn't fair, how I've showed up like this, but—" Joel swallowed and stared down at his hands "—my fiancée has a daughter close to...um, Henry's age, and I've come to understand how I failed you."

"It isn't about me," Chelsea said. "It never has been about me. It's about Henry and what he needs. You failed *him*, Joel."

"That's also why I'm here." Joel held up a cautionary hand and stood, reached into his back pocket and pulled out a sealed envelope. "It's a check, and it isn't much, but it's—"

"Tossing money at your son, rather than doing what's right and just." Dylan looked down at Chelsea and she knew, oh, she knew, that he was still fighting the urge to punch Joel.

Well, that made two of them.

"No. It's my attempt at showing how sorry I am," Joel said. "If I could reverse the years, I would make a different decision. I was a jerk back then. Too young and too selfish to care about anyone but myself." Joel's shoulders slumped by his admission. "I'm different now, and I wanted to give Henry something. To try to make it up to him. But, and you can believe this or not, I don't want to mess up his life."

Oh, God. He meant it. Every word of it.

And there went the rest of Chelsea's anger. She thought of her options, of what would be best for Henry as far as Joel went. And she couldn't allow a meeting between the two. Not now, or really, not in the near future, even if Joel wasn't leaving the country. Close to five years of zero contact was not erased by a solitary night of behaving responsibly, no matter how heartfelt and true she believed Joel's words to be.

"I accept your apology," she said, speaking slowly. "And someday, when Henry's older and can process the information correctly, I'll explain what you just have. If he wants to talk to you or meet you, we'll see where we're at, if it's a workable possibility. But, Joel, that's all I can do with this right now. Nothing more than that."

"That's fair. And more than I expected." Joel set the envelope on the seat of the chair he'd just vacated. "I'll be on my way now, no need to show me out."

He headed toward the outside door, and Chelsea couldn't

let him go without…something. "Joel," she said. "Wait. I think it would be okay for you to have a picture of Henry."

"Yeah?" Joel paused, turned around. "That would be great. Really great."

She ducked inside, chose a photo from her wallet and when she returned to the porch, handed it to Joel. "This was taken this past Christmas," she said. "And…well, if you text me an email address, I'll send you more photos here and there. If you'd like that."

Joel nodded, but his eyes were glued to the snapshot of Henry. "Look at him. Yeah, I really screwed up," he said, more to himself than to anyone else. Tucking the photo into his shirt pocket, he looked at Chelsea. His gaze held sorrow and, yes, regret. "Thank you. For keeping him safe and happy. I'll get that email address to you."

And with that, he was gone, and Chelsea's heart hung heavy with her own sorrow. She knew she'd made the right decision, but that didn't change the waste of it all.

"I'm proud of you. You handled that remarkably well," Dylan said, pulling her into his arms. She rubbed her cheek against his shirt, breathed in his clean, masculine scent and relaxed.

Just. Like. That.

Because, yes, she loved this man. But could he love her?

Several hours later, when the house was empty of all but those who lived there, save Dylan and Logan—who was in the living room, getting to know his half brother— Chelsea kissed Henry's cheek and quietly left the room. Her little boy was asleep, worn-out from the many ways Haley and Rachel had kept him occupied during Joel's visit.

The day had passed in a whirlwind of highs and lows, but rather than focus on the negative aspects, her heart was filled with only the good. Because in this city, in this house, she'd discovered the new fresh start she and Henry had so desperately needed. She'd found a family here, and they were a joy and a miracle. They were what she'd always yearned for, had always hoped to find.

And now she had them.

But the greater miracle was in the man named Dylan Foster. He'd poured his heart out to her today, had firmly stood by her—even when he'd been justifiably angry—as her world seemed to explode into smithereens, and… he'd called her *honey*.

In front of his mother, even.

Chelsea touched her lips with her fingers as she took the stairs, remembering their kisses and the passion that had followed. The way their bodies had merged together in heat and desire and then fulfillment. How being in Dylan's arms gave her the sensation of…coming home.

She had to believe he was the man meant for her, because otherwise, none of what she felt, none of what he'd said or done, none of what had occurred since she'd driven her dying car into Steamboat Springs, would make any type of sense.

The forces of fate had to be involved.

Now she had to take the final step. The one she'd avoided for so long—not just with Dylan, but with anyone. She had to share who she was, what had formed her, with him. So he could look inside her soul and decide for himself what he thought. Would he reject her?

The thought was crushing. Devastating. But this was a risk she had to take. If she didn't, if she stuck to her safe, sane world without ever knowing for certain, she would never forgive herself. Because the possibilities of what might occur if Dylan understood and accepted her, *loved* her, were…wondrous, and breath stealing, and of immeasurable significance.

Worth infinitely more than any number of diamonds or gold nuggets.

She peeked into the living room, but only saw Gavin, Logan and Haley. They were talking in easy, relaxed voices, and Gavin was smiling. That was good.

Since Dylan wasn't with them, she guessed he was waiting for her, and the most likely place, the most private place on the main floor, was the enclosed back porch. And yes, that was where she found him. Sitting in one of the chairs, legs stretched in front of him, arms cradled behind his head, and eyes closed. Oh, and with a wide, happy smile on his face.

Made her wonder what he was thinking of, dreaming of. Wishing for. Maybe, hopefully, something to do with her.

Clearing her throat, she waited for his eyes to open. When they did, she said, "He fell asleep right after the bedtime story. Thank you for reading to him." No, that wasn't quite right. She'd meant to say more. She'd meant to say *Thank you for loving my son*.

Dylan's brows shot up in surprise, maybe that she'd put it out there so clearly. "You're welcome, though I feel as if I should thank you. For…oh, let's start with bringing him into existence." He grinned. "And then for bringing him into my life."

Nervous trembles skittered up and down her spine, along her skin, and she figured the best chance she had of saying what she intended to say was to just do it. *Now.*

Before her litany of fears drove the words back down her throat. So she didn't sit, and she didn't give Dylan a heads-up. She just kept her gaze on his, opened her mouth and hoped like hell the right words, the ones she most needed to express, came out.

"There was a lot of yelling in my house," she said,

"when I was growing up. Condemning words, from both of my parents, and hurtful criticisms. I wasn't ever praised. I mean, I cannot ever remember being praised, for…anything. My interests were ridiculed, my dreams were made fun of, my fears were laughed at. No matter who I was, on any given day, it wasn't the right person. I wasn't—" she inhaled a fortifying breath "—the daughter they wanted."

Oh, Lord, this was rough. And it hurt, bringing those days to the forefront of her memory, remembering the girl she'd been. Remembering how very much she wanted her parents to love her. Appreciate her. See her and not wish for something, someone, she was not. How hard she'd tried and how often she'd failed.

But as hard, as painful as this was, she wasn't done. Not yet.

"My dad, he used to look at me as if I were an alien. Some creature unknown to him that he couldn't understand and, therefore, disliked. I spent half of my childhood trying to please him, and the other half walking on eggshells. Because, Dylan?" She said his name on purpose, to remind herself of why she was doing this. "I never knew what would set my father off. Lots would. But not every day, and not always the same things. And my mother, she just…passively went along with most of his tirades. Didn't step in. Didn't try to make it better."

Chelsea continued to look at Dylan, monitoring his expression—calm and focused, on her, on her story—as the words puked from her gut, from her soul. She said more than she ever had before, more than she'd believed she could, or would, when she'd started.

And this man she *knew* she loved watched her closely, with a dark and dangerous gleam in his eyes, and listened without interruption or one sign of impatience.

As she came to the end, she said, "When Henry was

born, my parents wanted me to give them guardianship. They said I was too young, too poor, too alone to raise him properly. I refused them, naturally, because even though I still wanted to please them, there wasn't any way I was going to allow my son to be raised as I was."

"What then?" Dylan asked quietly. Too quietly, she thought, almost as if she'd shocked the volume right out of him. "What did they do when you refused them?"

"Disowned us." A scared, choking laugh escaped. "Best thing they could've done, really, as I likely would've kept trying to fix all the problems they saw in me. Because in their eyes, I was always just a…a…failure."

Then, oh, God, then her legs buckled and she dropped to the floor. Trembles shot through her at breakneck speed, her pulse raced and her throat closed in. She couldn't speak. Couldn't breathe. Couldn't do anything but sit there as her body revolted, punishing her for…for ending her campaign of silence. For saying even one word of what lived inside her heart, her soul.

But then Dylan was there, on the floor with her, and his arms came around her and pulled her backward. Into him, into the safety and the warmth of home. Her home.

"You listen to me, Chelsea Bell," Dylan said, his voice strong and sure. "You are not a problem that needs fixing. Not even close. Your parents are the problem. Your parents failed you. *They* failed, baby, not you. Look at Henry if you don't believe me. He is incredible and loving and smart and funny…and he is that way due to you."

Pain she'd tried to repress for so long came to the surface as he spoke. It bubbled in her chest, it gurgled through her blood, it popped and hissed and crawled its way through her, one excruciating, unbearable inch at a time, until she truly and completely thought she would die from the agony. She gasped for air, tried to find a way to smother the hurt, as she had done for most of her life, to send it back into the recesses of her soul, to hide there—a silent enemy—so she wouldn't have to feel so damn much. So she could go back to…what?

Pretending she was fine?

No, no, no. She couldn't go back. Couldn't retreat into herself and keep her world as small and limited as she had. She…oh, wow, she deserved better. She wasn't a failure. She had taken what she'd been given and had done the best she could. Had fought and scraped her way through, one battle after another, and soaked up every bit of good she could get her hands on.

But she could do better than that. For herself, for Henry. And yes, for the man she loved. For Dylan. The burden that had weighed on her chest for so very long suddenly grew lighter, and lighter, and lighter yet, and then it floated away. Like one of Henry's hot-air balloons.

"I'm so damn grateful you shared this with me," Dylan was saying, his hold on her still secure, still strong. "I'm amazed by you, honey. By every part of what makes you… you."

"You're welcome," she said in a whisper, exhausted by all she'd done, all she felt. "I wanted you to know because I was afraid. Of what you'd think of me once you understood the reasons for how I am. If you'd…walk away, too. Like my parents. Like Joel."

"I'm not going anywhere. Not today, not tomorrow, not the next. Unless you decide you've had enough of me, I plan on sticking around."

Did that mean, could it mean, he loved her?

Maybe. Hopefully. But for now, she was happy enough, even secure enough, to believe his words as he said them. And since she knew, without doubt, that she'd never have her fill of Dylan Foster, there wasn't any hurry to rush their future or declare her love.

They'd get there, she was sure. Because she and Dylan

belonged together. Fate had brought her here, to him, and had put her smack-dab in the center of his arms.

Which was exactly where she was supposed to be.

Epilogue

Henry's stiff, starched shirt made his skin itch, and the long sleeves were too hot, and his dressing-up shoes pinched his toes. When he told Mommy, she said he could change later, but for weddings, people were supposed to wear their nice clothes.

He rubbed his back against his chair, trying to scratch the itches all the way gone, and squinted through the bright sun to watch Gavin and Haley become each other's family. 'Cause that was what getting married meant. Mommy had said that, too.

"Honey," Mommy whispered from next to him. She had on her nice clothes, but her dress had short sleeves, so she prolly wasn't hot. Or itchy. "Try to sit still, if you can."

"But I'm itchy!" he said. Oh. Maybe that was too loud, because the people around him laughed in their small voices. "But I'm itchy," he whispered. "And hot."

Dylan reached behind him to scratch his back, and he thought that was something a daddy would do. And he really, really wanted Dylan to be his daddy. He was the best person, 'cept for Mommy, that Henry had ever known in his whole life. He'd thought that Dylan *was* his daddy for a little while and that was why Mommy had brought him here for their fresh start.

He wasn't, though. Henry had asked and Dylan had told him the truth. He supposed he was glad that Dylan didn't lie, but his heart had hurt really bad then. Badder than falling from the swing. Badder than anything had ever hurt Henry before, even when he'd picked up the cactus plant Mommy used to have and all those tiny needles had stuck to his hand.

It made him sad, too. And mad. So mad he wanted to…to yell at his mommy for not picking Dylan to be his daddy. But he loved her and he knew if he yelled, she would cry. And he hated when she cried. That made his heart hurt, too, so he kept it all inside and pretended he was okay. He kind of thought Mommy knew that, though, because she'd started trying really hard—even harder than normal—to get him to smile and laugh.

Well, so did Dylan and Gavin and Haley and everyone else. His heart stopped hurting so much then, and he stopped being so mad and so sad. And that was when he started thinking about his mommy and Dylan getting married. Like Gavin and Haley were right now.

Mommy had said when they were driving in the car to see those crying babies that you got married when you loved someone and you wanted them to be your family. Henry loved Dylan more than root beer—which was his most favorite drink ever—and he loved him almost as much as he loved Mommy. And he wanted Dylan to be his daddy.

Since Dylan and Mommy were giving each other funny smiles, holding hands and kissing when they didn't think Henry was watching, they must love each other. Because that was what Gavin and Haley did. And Dylan was with him and Mommy almost every single day. They played games and went shopping and lots of other stuff, as if they *were* a family!

So Henry didn't understand why his mommy and Dylan weren't getting married. Seemed silly to him, to act like a family but not make it real.

Mommy was prolly waiting for Dylan to ask, and Dylan was prolly waiting for Mommy to ask, and that meant *no one* would ask. They'd just keep waiting forever and ever and ever, and they'd never be a real family and Dylan would never be Henry's daddy.

Henry squirmed in his chair and tried to think of what to do to stop the forever waiting. He thought so long and so hard, he missed all of Gavin and Haley's wedding. When everyone stood and clapped, he did, too. And when his mommy told him he could go play with the other kids if he wanted, he just found a table to sit at so he could keep thinking.

And then, when he finally decided what to do, it was time to eat the wedding food. He couldn't eat very much, though, because his tummy felt funny. Kind of like when he spun in circles really, really fast. Henry knew he wasn't sick or anything gross like that, he was just getting worried about what he was going to do. About what Mommy and Dylan would say.

But this was about making them all a *real* family. And that was so, so, so important. More important than how his tummy felt.

And he didn't want to wait anymore. Remembering something he'd seen on TV, Henry picked up his spoon and his glass of root beer and stood up on his chair, which wobbled a little at first. Mommy saw him right away and tugged at Dylan's shirt, so he looked at Henry then, too.

Henry hit the glass with the spoon, but it didn't make

the ringing bell noise like on TV, and nobody but Mommy and Dylan seemed to notice. He swallowed really hard and in his biggest voice said, "Everyone stop talking! And everyone look at me, 'cause I have something important to say!"

"Um, Henry," Mommy said, starting to stand. "Maybe this isn't the—"

"Oh, I don't know, honey," Dylan said, winking at Henry. "He said it was important. Maybe let him talk and see what this is about?"

She nodded and sat back down, but she had those worry lines around her mouth that Henry didn't like. "Okay, sweetie, go ahead."

"Mommy," Henry said, starting with her, since he'd known her ever since he was a baby, "I think you are the best mommy in the world and I love you very much. You bake real good and you tell the best stories and…and your laugh makes my heart happy. Even if I'm sad first."

"Thank you, sweetie." She blinked and her worry lines became smiling ones. He liked those lines a lot. "And I think you're the best son in the world, and I love you, too. More than you'll ever know. Was that what you wanted to say?"

"Yes, but there's more. *Lots* more." Then, still using his superbig voice, he said, "Dylan, I think you *could* be the best daddy in the world, but you're not my daddy, so it's hard to say for hundred percent sure. I'm prolly ninety-two percent there right now, and that's pretty good!"

There was lots of chuckling all around him, but all Henry cared about was that his mommy and Dylan were laughing. And they were. Dylan was even holding Mommy's hand.

"You're right, kid," Dylan said. His eyes were real shiny. As though he was happy. "Ninety-two percent is pretty darned good. Thank you for—"

"But I don't wanna wait forever and ever for you to be my real daddy." Henry's big voice sounded weird to him now, so he changed to his medium one. "'Cause I love you, Dylan, and I think you love me and my mommy. And I think she loves you. But no one's asked *anyone* to be married yet and that's why I'm gonna ask, so we can… get this ball rolling!"

More laughter, but not from Mommy and Dylan. They looked surprised but not mad. Other people were talking, though. Someone from behind Henry said, "Look how cute he is!"

And someone else said, "This might be the most romantic proposal ever."

Henry smiled as hard as he could and stood up straighter. "Mommy, I don't have a diamond ring or any ring at all, but I am asking you to marry Dylan anyway." He breathed in and out real fast. "And, Dylan, will you marry my mommy and be my daddy? If you say yes, you'll have to buy Mommy a really pretty ring with a really big diamond, because Mommy should have the best."

They *had* to say yes. They just had to, because if they said no, he thought his heart would hurt even badder than that day at the park. It might even break, and he didn't think any doctor anywhere could fix a broken heart.

Dylan looked at Mommy, and Mommy looked at Dylan, but neither one of them said yes or no. They just looked at each other and that made Henry more nervous, and his tummy started to feel worse. But then Dylan slid off the chair and knelt in front of Mommy. He reached into his jacket and pulled out a little black box. When he opened it, there *was* a ring there!

And it had a very big diamond.

"Honey, your son sort of stole the show here, and I wasn't actually going to propose today," Dylan said. "But I bought this ring last week and have been carrying it around with me ever since. In case the proper moment presented itself, and I'd say it just has."

"Oh, Dylan, really? This seems so fast, and—" she blinked, like three million hundred times "—and this isn't rational, you know. In any way, shape or form."

"It isn't reasonable, either. But, Chelsea, from the second I found you and Henry close to freezing in that car of yours, everything changed in my world. You became my world." Dylan took the ring out of the box and held it out to Mommy. "I love you, and Lord, I hope you love me, too, and I hope you can see the logic in our son's very eloquent words. Because we are a family. And I don't much feel like waiting forever, either."

"So we're just going to throw away the rational and the reasonable here, huh?" She sounded funny, as if she was talking underwater, and her eyes were all soft. "In one fell swoop?"

"Mommy," Henry said in his really big-big-big voice. "All you have to do is say yes! Please say yes!"

Dylan winked. "You heard him, honey. How can you say no now?"

She laughed then. "I don't want to wait forever, either. Because I absolutely am in love with you and because you *are* Henry's father. So…yes, I accept your proposal, Dylan." She tipped her head up to look at Henry. "And yes, my darling son, I accept yours, as well."

There was a bunch of cheering and lots and lots of clapping, and Mommy and Dylan were kissing, and Henry didn't think his heart had ever been so happy in his whole entire life.

He had a daddy. The *best* daddy ever.

The sun had just started to set, and in all ways, the day had been a joy.

Surprising, for the family and friends attending the

nuptials, and for Chelsea, as well. She was engaged to Dylan. She was to be his wife, and he her husband. Perhaps not completely rational, given the timing, but beautifully and exquisitely…perfect.

And to think her son's bravery, his tenacious and never-give-up attitude, had—as he'd said—gotten the ball rolling. Oh, from the looks of her gorgeous ring, Dylan would've proposed sooner rather than later, but it wouldn't have been today.

And she was so very, very happy for the blessings, the miracles of today.

"You're looking rather contemplative there, honey," Dylan said, offering her his hand. "I hope you're not having second thoughts."

"Just the opposite," she said, putting her hand in his. "I'm thinking that there isn't a woman alive who is as fortunate as I am."

And oh, was she ever lucky. Dylan understood her. He'd looked deep into her soul, directly at her scars, and not only hadn't he retreated, but he'd stepped even closer. It was, Chelsea decided, yet another miracle in a day brimming with them.

"Come with me," Dylan said, tugging her along the side of the house. He wanted to dance with his soon-to-be wife, whisper sweet nothings into her ear and tell her repeatedly how very much he loved her. "We're going to dance."

The outdoor deck had been strung with sparkly lights, and soft music played in the background. Mr. and Mrs. Daugherty—jeez, his baby sister was married!—were already dancing, with Haley's head cushioned on Gavin's shoulder. They were spectacular.

But so was Chelsea.

When they reached the deck, he swung her into his arms, pulled her in close, and they began to dance. Her scent—that sexy mix of orange, honey and jasmine— wove around him, and he thought, again, of how intelligent his heart was, for recognizing this woman so quickly. For being so insistent that he had no choice but to pay attention and claim her as his.

Because she was, indeed, his. And he was hers.

Dylan brought his hand to her face, tucked her hair behind her ear and whispered, "I love you, Chelsea. And I want to get married soon. As soon as you're willing to become Chelsea Foster, and then, if you're okay with the idea, I want to adopt Henry."

More of a necessity, actually.

She stepped back, and there were tears—of joy, of pleasure, of love—shimmering in the depths of her gorgeous blue eyes. "How soon?" she asked. "Because I'm ready to be your wife now. And of course you'll adopt Henry, because he's your son, and we need to make it official."

At that moment, Henry—his smart, brave, ice-flying *son*—ran onto the deck and, spying them, came to a dead halt at their sides. He looked at Dylan. "I want to know," he said, his voice unsure, "if I can start calling you Daddy now or if I have to wait until after we all get married?"

"Do you want to call me Daddy now?" Could his heart hold any more love, any more pride, than it already did? Dylan didn't see how that would be possible. "Because if you do, then yes…I would be most honored. And—"

"Okay, Daddy." Henry's smile was so large, so bright, it outshone the sun. "I was thinking that we should talk about adding babies to this family. Not right away, and not two at a time because that's too much crying, but maybe in a year, I'd like to have a brother or a sister."

And there, Dylan thought, was his answer. Yes. His heart could indeed hold more.

Laughing, he let go of Chelsea and pulled Henry in between them so they could dance together. As the family they were always meant to be. *His* family. His…everything.

Damn, life was good.

* * * * *

MILLS & BOON®

The Thirty List

At thirty, Rachel has slid down every ladder she has ever climbed. Jobless, broke and ditched by her husband, she has to move in with grumpy Patrick and his four-year-old son.

Patrick is also getting divorced, so to cheer themselves up the two decide to draw up bucket lists. Soon they are learning to tango, abseiling, trying stand-up comedy and more. But, as she gets closer to Patrick, Rachel wonders if their relationship is too good to be true...

Order yours today at
www.millsandboon.co.uk/Thethirtylist

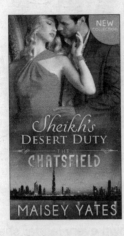

MILLS & BOON®

Cherish™

EXPERIENCE THE ULTIMATE RUSH OF FALLING IN LOVE

A sneak peek at next month's titles...

In stores from 19th June 2015:

- **The Millionaire's True Worth** – Rebecca Winters *and*
  His Proposal, Their Forever – Melissa McClone

- **A Bride for the Italian Boss** – Susan Meier *and*
  The Maverick's Accidental Bride – Christine Rimme

In stores from 3rd July 2015:

- **The Earl's Convenient Wife** – Marion Lennox *and*
  How to Marry a Doctor – Nancy Robards Thompso

- **Vettori's Damsel in Distress** – Liz Fielding *and*
  Daddy Wore Spurs – Stella Bagwell

Available at WHSmith, Tesco, Asda, Eason, Amazon and Apple

Just can't wait?
Buy our books online a month before they hit the shops!
visit www.millsandboon.co.uk

These books are also available in eBook format!